THERAPY DIALOGUE

A session by session therapy dialogue with a client who went through the self-actualization and self-growth processes.

Roya R. Rad, MA, PsyD

Disclaimer

The publisher and the author make an effort to give valid information to the public, however, they make no guarantee with respect to the accuracy or completeness of the contents of the books published. Science is unlimited and there are many facts yet to be discovered and improved upon, as the world expands. The information that SKBF Publishing presents to the public can only be used as a personal enhancing device for building a healthy life style. The reader is always responsible for using the information the best possible way according to his or her unique needs, environment and personality. Books, lectures, websites and other forms of self help tools are general and valuable tools for a person looking for self education but, sometimes, they are more like statistical information. They will give us a general idea about most people but we have to remember that each of us is a unique individual and treatment for our healing process would have to be administered accordingly.

Printed in Victoria, BC, Canada.
ISBN: 978-1-4269-2637-2 (sc)
ISBN: 978-1-4269-2638-9 (hc)
Library Congress Control Number: 2010900471

Our mission is to efficiently provide the world's finest, most comprehensive book publishing service, enabling every author to experience success. To find out how to publish your book, your way, and have it available worldwide, visit us online at www.trafford.com
Trafford rev. 1/12/2010
Published by SKBF Publishing
(Self Knowledge Base/Foundation Publishing)
43803 Michener Dr.
Ashburn VA 20147
www.SKBFPublishing.com
First Edition:
copyright © 2008 by SKBF Publishing, Ashburn, Virginia
All rights reserved. No part of this book may be reproduced, or used in any form or by any means, electronic, mechanical, photocopying, microfilming, recording, or otherwise, without written permission from the publisher.

Published in USA by SKBF Publishing www.SKBFPublishing.com
Disclaimer: The publisher and the author make no guarantee with respect to the accuracy or completeness of the contents of this book.
Edited by: Walter L. Kleine, Kleine Editorial Services.

Trafford
PUBLISHING www.trafford.com
North America & international
toll-free: 1 888 232 4444 (USA & Canada)
phone: 250 383 6864 ♦ fax: 812 355 4082

Contents

Dedication

I dedicate this book to my two sons, Paul (Parham) & Peter (Pedram) who have thought me what it means to have an unconditional love. In addition, I dedicate this book to the true lovers of existence who are craving to learn the deeper truth beyond the shallow, to apply what they learn, and to try to improve their life as well as that of others.

Therapy Dialogue

A session by session therapy dialogue with a client who went through the self-actualization and self-growth processes.

This book walks the reader through the process of therapy. In a step by step guide, it discusses what it means to live a life of "false self" and how to find a sense of "real self". It discusses a wide variety of issues like anxiety, family relationship, romantic relationship, negative behaviors and emotions and how to get rid of them, how to get to our full potential, what happiness really means, what is the difference between love and anxious attachment, what is assertiveness, how to process suppressed memories, and how to be able to see deeper into people's intention not just behavior.

Introduction

To understand the content of this book and how the process of therapy worked for the person whose therapy is documented here, one needs to become familiar with the concept of self-actualization. This concept has been explained in my other book, Rumi & Self Psychology (Psychology of Tranquility), and the reader will find some of the same subjects repeated here.

This client's goal was to become self-actualized, and to be purified of the heavy and harmful baggage she had carried with her throughout her life; the baggage of negative emotions, thoughts, blockages, and unattended needs. We will refer to the Maslow's pyramid for the concept of self-actualization. This pyramid can help explain human motivation and personal development in life. We, humans have both physical and emotional needs and are motivated by satisfying these needs in life. Our most basic needs are inborn and have evolved over many years. It is only when the lower needs of physical and emotional well-being are satisfied or compensated that we are able to take care of the higher ones.

Maslow's hierarchy of needs is represented as a pyramid with the more primitive needs at the bottom and the more advanced ones on the top. This hierarchy is portrayed as a pyramid of five main levels, each with its own characteristics. The author has added two more levels to this pyramid. Walking through this pyramid seems something like walking through a path, a very personal path. It also seems like going through school and seeking a higher degree. The higher the degree, the more difficult it gets, but at the same time the person has more skills, intelligence, and strength to deal with the difficulties.

By graduating from each level and going to the next, it seems like one's mind and core being are expanding. We can also relate the pyramid to climbing up the mountain. Not everyone can get to the top, since going to the top needs strength, motivation, and determination. It also needs strong muscles that are built during practice and training. With each step up, muscles contract and expand, getting ready for the next one. As one climbs higher up the mountain, she sees everything down below with a more expanded vision.

The same applies with a person's psych. As one goes up the pyramid of growth, one gets stronger and more evolved, and is ready for the next level. During the process of self-growth, one has to be aware and familiar with these levels to be able to aim toward them. Otherwise, a whole life could be wasted living at the lower ones.

One must take note of the fact that how each person's needs are met, and at what stage of life that need becomes a priority, is a truly personal factor that relates to the person's characteristics, the environment she was raised in, and the predisposed factors she came into this world with. However, it is each person's responsibility to become aware of these needs, so she is able to go through each in a healthy way.

During the process of self-growth, some go through a stage much faster than others, and some pass through a stage and come back to it again, later in life. For example, one might have sexual needs, but may also have strong personal values that in order to be sexually intimate with a person, one must bond with that person on deeper levels first, emotionally or spiritually, or even perhaps be in a long-term relationship with him or her, or get married, before having a sexual relationship. Now, if this person is unable to find the right partner but still has the sexual needs, he or she must find other ways to satisfy this need in healthy ways, rather than letting it block his or her growth or letting this unmet need turn into damaging behaviors. This way, the individual is able to stand up to her values while she is not jamming him or herself because of unmet needs. That is why being aware of needs instead of denying that they exist is a productive way of going about the self-growth process.

To refer back to the levels of the pyramid, the four lower levels (survival/physiological, security/safety, love/belonging/social acceptance, and self-esteem) are grouped together as deficiency needs, and are all related, one way or another, to physiological needs. The top level (self-actualization) is termed a growth need, and is related to psychological needs. Going from the lowest level to the top, the first level of needs, survival and physiological, are things like breathing, food, water, sleep, homeostatic which is the ability of an organism to maintain an internal equilibrium, and excursion.

The second level of needs, security and safety needs, are things like security of body, employment, resources, morality, family, health, and property.

The third level of needs, social acceptance, love, and belonging needs, are things like acceptance, friendship, family, and sexual intimacy.

The fourth level of needs, self-esteem, are things like confidence, achievement, and respect for and by others.

The fifth level of needs, self-actualization, are morality, spontaneity, creativity, productivity, lack of prejudice, and respect for others and nature.

The basic concept of the pyramid is that once the lower needs are met, the individual can move up to the next higher need. Once an individual passes one level, that level's needs will no longer be prioritized, though they may still exist. On the other hand, if a lower set of needs is persistently unmet and neglected for a long time, the individual will temporarily re-prioritize those needs by dropping down to that level until those lower needs are realistically fulfilled again. Natural growth forces continuously generate upward movement in the hierarchy, unless basic needs remain unmet indefinitely.

The first four levels of the pyramid, which Maslow called the "deficiency needs" or "D needs," are the ones that the individual feels anxious about if they are not met. Besides, and after, fulfilling the most basic physiological and safety needs, humans need to have a sense of social belonging. This is commonly an emotionally-based relationship. Everyone needs to feel a sense of belonging and acceptance, whether from a large social group like cultural, professional, sports, or religious groups; or from small groups like family, partner, mentor, colleagues, and close friends. All humans need to love and be loved by others, sexually and non-sexually. When these needs are not met, and if the individual is unable to find productive ways to cope with the unmet needs, the individual may become vulnerable to a feeling of loneliness, anxiety, and depression. Other symptoms may be addictions, overwork, or imbalances in any aspect of one's life.

This need for belonging can often conquer the physiological and security needs, depending on the strength of peer and social pressures, and the strength of the person dealing with these pressures. An example would be a person who does not eat a healthy diet, trying to look a certain way for a feeling of belonging to, or getting approval from, a certain group.

During the forth level of the pyramid, self-esteem, individuals have a need to be respected by others, learn to respect their self, and learn to respect others. At this level, humans have a need to be acknowledged, feel a sense of giving, feel accepted and self-valued, and be in a profession or hobby. Unmet needs at this level may result in low self-esteem, inferiority complexes, or an inflated sense of self-importance and superiority. At this level, there are two inner layers of esteem that have to be distinguished.

The lower layer of esteem is the need people are trying to fulfill through fame, respect, and success; that is, a feeling of "being good" in the eyes of others. This is a less mature form of esteem.

The higher level of esteem, on the other hand, consists of an inner sense of confidence, competence, and achievement, without the need for the approval of others. The lower layer of self-esteem is generally regarded as less advanced, because it is conditional upon other people. Individuals at this level need reassurance and respect from others to feel good about themselves, because of lower esteem. For example, they may seek fame or success to please others and get attention, which makes the feeling dependent on others. However, at the higher level, confidence, competence, and achievement only need one person. How that person feels about him or herself is important. How everyone else feels about one is insignificant to one's own feeling of success.

People with low self-esteem should learn to accept themselves on the inside to be able to see themselves in a more realistic light. To be able to do that, they have to learn to know themselves, their strengths, their weaknesses, and their limitations.

At the higher layer of esteem, cognitive and artistic needs are also a part of what the individual may be in search of.

Maslow believed that humans, at this level, have the need to improve their intelligence, knowledge, beautiful imagery, discovering nature, and observing their surroundings, which may result in learning to explore, discover, and create at the higher level of self-esteem needs.

So far, we've discussed basic and intermediate needs, even at the self-esteem level. The following levels are termed the higher needs.

At this level, which is termed self-actualization, one needs to become, as the term indicates, self-actualized. Self-actualization is the instinctive need of humans to make the most of their capacity, and to make every effort to the best they can. It is the intrinsic growth of what is already in the organism.

We will discuss characteristics of self-actualizers in more detail in the following chapters. To discuss them briefly, some characteristics of self-actualized people are that they embrace the facts and realities of the world, rather than denying or avoiding them, are spontaneous, creative, good problem-solvers who use reason rather than emotion, focus on the solution, not the problem, and appreciate life in general, with all its ups and downs, have a system of morality that is fully internalized and independent of external authority, and are aware, open, honest, free, and trustworthy in every aspect.

Finally, there is a seventh and final layer of the pyramid, which comes after a person has become self-actualized. This is called the self-transcendence or self-transformation level. This is where the person becomes her true self. Some term this as the ultimate spirituality. It is worth noting that only a very small percentage of people can get to this level, Some psychologists estimate that only 2% of population reaches self-actualization, and an even smaller number of people reach the self-transcendence level. This is not because they do not have the ability to do so, but because they get trapped in fulfilling the lower-level needs of the pyramid, and suppress, avoid, or deny their higher needs.

At the self-transcendence level, many people have peak experiences which are unifying and ego-transcending, which bring a sense of purpose and integration to the individual. This level may be what many prophets and people who affected life in a positive way have reached. It is where a feeling of enlightenment comes more naturally than any other feelings. At this state, the individual has her rational and emotional sides balanced and her emotions in control.

It may be worth mentioning that many people who consider themselves spiritual or religious may have been attracted to those beliefs because of the lower levels of needs, like physiological, security, social acceptance, or self-esteem. Some examples would be a person who imitates her parents' spiritual or religious beliefs without knowing why, or how to apply these to her self-growth;

or another person who becomes religious in the hopes of having a better lifestyle or health, either here or in an afterlife, or the one who becomes religious to become a part of a bigger group to get some form of support.

All these people seem to be looking at a bigger picture, the unknown, one that will give them hope during hard times and will keep them motivated and determined to move on and have their needs met. These forms of spirituality or religiousness, if used in a healthy and balanced way, have been shown to be beneficial to the individual, but are not the self-transcendent type of spirituality that was placed at the top of the pyramid. One has to be able to see the difference between the two in order to be able to make progress up the ladder of self-discovery and growth.

After all, many may believe what Carl Jung believed, that the main purpose for humans' lives is to recognize their "self." Yet, many of us do everything but that. This book is dedicated to those who want to accomplish this. We have to remember that there is no quick fix; growing and healing should be done with love, patience, determination, knowledge, applying the knowledge, and hope. A quick fix will be temporary. It will not restore the self to health. It's like a pain reliever that does not cure. It just takes the pain away for a short time.

For people who are looking to do some serious work and want to reach the ultimate level of inner freedom, there are no quick fixes, but a continuous journey.

Sara is one of those people.

The story of Sara can be used as an example for all of us who want to go up the pyramid of self-discovery and self-growth. How far we want to go is a personal decision and choice, one that cannot be imposed, nor can it be imitated. An "I" journey is one that belongs to all of us, uniquely and individually. Once we realize that we are so much more than our animalistic needs, we will stop chasing them for too long and will move on to discover the deeper side of us.

During the course of life, even when we achieve all the material, animalistic and primitive needs, we still may feel that something is missing; a part of our essence that we feel is not complete.

What is it?

What is it that humans are searching for?

Could it be that this missing part is the "I" sense, the one that we need to get to know to be able to experience?

We cannot just read about it. We cannot imitate others. We have to experience it, personally.

Whatever we have achieved during the course of life is supposed to be an outside tool for us to get to know this "I," but somehow we get lost in the process of achieving these tools. We identify ourselves as the tools, forgetting that we are so much more.

These tools can be very useful for the process of growth. Tools like education, wealth, intelligence, talent, or others are important, but at times it seems like we get trapped in achieving these tools, and the very tool that was supposed to help us with our self-growth will become a block that prevents us from developing in other areas of life to its full extent.

We may focus too much on gaining these tools and maintaining them, identifying ourselves as them. For example, we say, I am a doctor, a businessman, a son, a politician, a mother, a housewife… and before we know it, we have defined our life in those terms, and wasted a large part of our life chasing them, without them giving us any sense of learning anything about who we truly are. In many instances, they become the means for being dragged into denial and avoidance of the true world and the meaning of life.

During the course of self-growth, we have to make continuous progress and change for a more expanded and evolved being. We have to move forward, get through one level, get stable and move to the next. We have to wash away all the dust and throw away the dirty baggage to find our true value.

We all have a diamond buried inside, the innocent child who is still waiting to be nurtured. We need to learn to recognize that sense of identity. After all, we're supposed to be the most advanced creatures because we're the only creatures that can create with advancement. What this means is that our creation keeps on getting improved. Animals can create, but their creation seems to stay stable. For example, a spider can design a very sophisticated web, but this has not changed for as long as spiders have been making them.

Humans, on the other hand, are constantly making progress in many areas of life. How is it that we can do that? Is it our five senses? It can't be, because these five senses are weaker than those of most animals. Is it our brain? We can't deny that our brain is advanced, and has evolved greatly since the beginning of human's creation, but then it takes one little push for it to get totally mixed up, one stroke and it loses all its memory.

There has to be something more.

What is it?

Let's look for it by walking through the process of self-discovery. Let's throw out the old habits if they're not productive, and learn new ones. Let's move forward, one step at a time. Let's be open to risk-taking and making new decisions with reason, rather than acting impulsively. Let's not be ignorant anymore. Let's not be scared of change, because with change comes growth. Let's move out of that comfort zone and climb up the mountain of self-growth. It gets easier and more joyous if we walk together.

To be able to climb the mountain of self-actualization, we need to pay attention to the following guidelines.

We need to know our limits before starting the process, and to become familiar with our motivation.

We need to ask ourselves, "Why it is that I want to do this?"

Another important factor is awareness of our physical, mental, and coral (deep layers of a human being) limits. This is an important aspect of being able to know how much we can push our limits without overstretching them. Overstretching can be as negative as under-stretching. The other important guideline is listening to our intuition; if something looks too good to be true, it probably is. We need to learn to ask for help and advice from those who have the knowledge to help us, we need to be very particular about who we trust and ask for help, and we need to do this based on quality, not quantity. Just because someone has this many followers does not make her a qualified and trustworthy person.

We need to learn the necessary skills to climb up the mountain of self-discovery and self-actualization. Each stage needs new skills, which are enhancements of the older ones. We need to learn what works and what does not, so that we will not make the same mistake more than once. We need to climb with light baggage. We should only pack what is needed, and leave behind or throw away the rest. This baggage could be anything from our own harmful habits, thoughts, or behaviors; or emotionally draining people who constantly want to drag us down with their words or actions. Unneeded tools that will be a burden should be discarded, so we can walk with ease.

Remember Einstein's physics law; the less the mass, the more the speed.

We should be determined, ready for work, focused, motivated, and aware. We should also be ready to take risks, if needed. While climbing up, with each muscle contraction comes a muscle expansion, and that makes our muscles stronger for the next move upward. The same formula applies to our core being. It's a beautiful design that works the same with everything.

Session 1

When Sara came to therapy, she was 34 years old, beautiful, intelligent, anxious, and seemed very eager to talk. She started to bond quickly with the therapist and the therapy room. In the therapy room, in Sara's eyes, the therapist was the one with power, and she had come to her for help. It was easy for Sara to open up, and she revealed information about her life that might take some many sessions to be able to talk about. It seemed like she had been holding these unspoken words for such a long time, and they were buried inside her. She said that they were burning her and she felt helpless, but was still full of hope. While she was talking, the therapist found herself being dragged into Sara's being. She saw a unique deepness in Sara, a beauty in her essence, a mystery in her eyes, and wisdom in her mind.

The first session was a typical time of rapport building—until Sara suddenly started to sob. A sob was not expected, but then again, in therapy, many things happen unexpectedly. She stared at the therapist with her brown eyes, eyes with so many untold stories. She took a deep breath, her hands shaking, her eyes full of tears, one tear after the other started to come out. It seemed like these tears have been held back for such a long time. Her tears were so full of meaning that it seemed like they would burn the observer's heart. They came out slowly and gently at first, then faster and faster. They chased each other, and it seemed like they could not wait to be out and were sensing and celebrating freedom.

After giving Sara some time to relax, we had an introduction in which we discussed the methods that were going to be implemented during our work together. We also discussed the fact that what we were about to have was more of a coaching relationship that included a lot of therapy, and how it was multimodal, meaning that a combination of techniques were going to be used, rather than one technique, and a lot of other general information.

After that, Sara started to talk. Her voice was full of pain, yet full of hope, strength, and joy. Sara reported that she'd been working on the process of self-discovery for more than a year before seeking a therapist. She said that she'd done a lot of reading about it, and had made a number of major changes in her life. But, she said, she needed an extra boost to go further, and that she had many unanswered questions related to herself and her life.

She said that, since she was a teenager, she had always been very interested in things like spirituality, the meaning of life, and deeper answers to life. As a result, she joined many spiritual and religious groups, mosques, churches, etc., searching for an answer, but they did not satisfy her. She found, however, many scholars' books and other information that were very helpful in her increasing her knowledge, but it wasn't until she really turned the camera on herself, looking deeply into her being, that she realized she needed to make major changes, and that the process of self-discovery was not about imitating others, but about learning from others and applying what was learned uniquely to one's self.

These are the main parts of what went on during the sessions with Sara. As the reader goes through these sessions, she will be walked through a process of personal purification, growth, and advancement. The same process can be applied to each individual who is serious about making changes. During the first session, after initial small-talk and rapport building, we started the process.

Therapist: So, it seems like you have a lot of untold stories, and I'm looking forward to hearing about them. Let's start by telling me what brings you in for therapy.

Sara: Well, I have many reasons for seeking therapy. First, I want to learn more about myself in a meaningful way, rather than based on unreasonable beliefs. I've been to many spiritual classes, but none of them have been able to totally help me with what I am searching for. It seems like a repetition of words. I need to learn to apply these words to myself, or they will only be a series of words and nothing else. Many of the spiritual classes I've been to have given me good information, but I never learned what I was supposed to do with the information. I've read many books related to science, spirituality, psychology, nature, physics, the cosmos, and other books, and always want to know *why*, based on facts and reason, rather than someone's personal ideas. I know there's much more to this than I see, and I thought you would be the person to go to.

My second reason for coming to therapy is that it's hard for me to open up to others, even my friends and family, and I needed to find a knowledgeable person who is like an observer rather than a judge, to see me and hear me, and just be with me. Also, I'm going through the process of divorce. Though I've had many challenges in my life, this seems to be the most challenging one, and I need to talk it over with someone, not just anyone, someone who will understand and observe, rather than judge and misinterpret.

Then she took a deep breath and continued:

Sara: Sometimes, I feel so lonely these days. I'm surrounded by many people, but it seems like this sense of loneliness is getting deeper, and that this is a part of my life I have to walk by myself. Sometimes it seems heartrending and intimidating. I've had many challenges in my life, and have worked so very hard to get to where I am today. But, it seems like others, I mean one specific person, wants to take it all away from me. And that one person is after me not because I did something to hurt him, but because I did so much for him. When I decided I wasn't going to do it any more, he got irritated and reacted to it in a very immature way, attacking me from every possible angle. He was doing it so passively that even he himself seemed to believe his own denial, sometimes. He was like a child, but not an innocent child. He was more of a dangerous child, who is out to get you. Defending myself and my children took a lot of energy. I had to learn a lot of new skills I didn't have before. I wasn't used to being attacked, since I'm a peace-seeker, and usually avoided altercations before this, but it seemed like I've had enough of it.

I asked her to elaborate.

Sara: Well, I'm going through a divorce. This divorce is something I've wanted for a long time, but never dared to take steps to accomplish. I was drawn into something hurtful that I wasn't able to get out of. I didn't know how to get out, or if I ever could. I felt like I had poisonous food stuck in my throat, but was unable to spit it out; I felt like choking during my married years. I know that may seem like a harsh sentence, but that's how I felt. My way of thinking, and putting others ahead of me, made me live with this feeling for more than fifteen years, up to a point where I sensed being close to self-destruction if I didn't do anything about it. That's when I took the steps to do something.

Of course, by self-destruction I don't mean suicide. What I mean is an emotional blockage. The sad part is that I pretended that this poison was a nourishing food. I pretended so much that I believed it on the surface, but deep down inside I knew how I felt. Why is it Doctor, why did I pretend like that, why did I not do anything about it for so many years? What's wrong with me?

Therapist: Well, it seems to me that you're referring to a comfort zone that was damaging to you and your emotional as well as focal state of being. And my focal I mean your core being, your essence.

Sometimes we, as humans, stay in this comfort zone and are not ready to get out, even though our deep understanding knows that it's not being productive, or may even be damaging. The basic reason for it is fear. We fear the unknown. We fear what might be outside our comfort zone. At least, here, in this comfort zone, we know it, we are used to it, even if it's not productive for us. If we change it and move one step higher, we don't know what might be waiting for us. We see many challenges, and sometimes we aren't ready to face them. Somehow, we feel weak, we feel insecure, we don't feel we deserve better. This could be due to low self-esteem, which is a result of inner voices that have been imposed upon us through our childhood and by our environment. There could be many reasons for the same problem. Once we get to know each other better, we may get a better idea as to what yours might be. Let's go back to your story. Tell me what's on your mind.

Sara: I think I'll focus on my marriage and the divorce first. Is that okay?

Therapist: Whatever feels right to *you*.

Sara: Okay, as I was saying, I'm going through a divorce right now. My marriage was not something I wanted. It was more like an escape from a lonely childhood. I also felt like my dad, emotionally, forced me into marrying. My dad always made me feel like women have certain roles they have to fulfill; very limited roles. Women have to be married at a certain age, or something must be innately wrong with them. I didn't feel much love and support from my mom, either. Therefore, I saw this marriage as an opportunity to escape from a lonely place. There were many women in my family who married for that exact same reason, so it didn't seem abnormal at the time. During the first few months of my marriage, I knew that I'd made a mistake. My husband was just so different from what I was attracted to in a man. It seemed like our personalities were so different from each other in many ways. His behavior was the exact opposite of what captivated me in a man, and his beliefs were nothing close to what my beliefs were. For one thing, it seemed to me that he did not even *have* a belief. He seemed to take in everyone else's beliefs and change them constantly, according to who was around and who he wanted to impress. He was just so…

Then came a quietness, and all of a sudden her crying started again. I let her be and gave her some tissues. She stared at the floor, tears coming down. Deep breaths followed, and then quietness.

> **Sara:** You know Doctor, I feel like I wasted a large portion of my youth. Many years of my life were washed away from me. I was unhappy, but what makes me feel mad at myself is that through all those years I was pretending to be something I was not. It seemed like I put a mask on, and believed my own mask. It seemed like I wanted to keep others happy and proud of me, rather than keeping myself happy, because...

I noticed her feeling overwhelmed, and offered her a glass of water.

> **Sara:** Yes, that would be great Thank you.

When I brought her water, I noticed her meditating. I respected that and waited until she was ready. When I sat down, she seemed to be ready, too.

> **Sara:** You know doctor, it seemed like I shattered a portion of my life trying to please others. My father, my mother, my husband, my this, my that, what's the point? What about impressing and pleasing myself and my core being? What am I getting for working so hard to please others? Why am I still like a child who needs to please?
>
> I've thought a lot about myself. I've come to realize that some of my beliefs were irrational, and very damaging to me; that extra baggage I was carrying with me, the extra baggage of irrational thinking and damaging behavior. I'm in the process of changing them, but it's very difficult. I read about self-discovery, and investigated a lot about

these concepts, and started to think deeply about mine. Can you explain the concept of irrational thinking? What is it, where do we get it, and how do we change it? I want to hear from you and your point of view and knowledge.

Therapist: Sure, irrational thinking is a part of many of us. Many times we have a belief and don't know why we have it. It's been imposed upon us by family, friend, teachers, media, or surroundings. We've never come to question these beliefs, some of which might be harmful and destructive. We react impulsively, sometimes, to these beliefs, acting in a way that results in our dissatisfaction with life, and, in the process, losing our balanced sense of self. Some of these beliefs may have been useful at a certain time and place, but they may not be useful any more. But we, through imitation, just keep repeating them, not once questioning their validity, *today*, and their relation to our personal values and lifestyle. We'll talk about this some more, and I'll give you some work to do to go through the process of challenging irrational beliefs and replacing them with more rational ones. This will encourage you to respect your true sense of self, and the messages it gives you, rather than what others tell you to do. We will do this soon. We all have what we need, already built inside us. Most of us, however, don't pay attention to it. Now, let's go back to your story. You said that you had a mask on. In Jungian psychotherapy, we call this a persona, and we'll talk about it more in the future. Now, let's see where this persona has come from, and let's look at your childhood. How about going according to your chronological age, starting with your childhood memories, good or bad? Tell me the first thing that comes to your mind about your childhood.

After a pause, Sara started to cry, a cry that brought about the same burning sensation in the observer. Her cry gave the observer the deepest form of compassionate connection to her. Her cry had a sense of pride to it, and there seemed to be so many unspoken words waiting to get out. I let her be, sat down quietly, and waited until she was ready to talk.

Sara: I think I've found my sanctuary here in your office, my safe place to talk, a place where I won't be judged. You know, this is the number one fear of everyone I talk to; fear of being judged by others. Because, let's admit it, most of us are ignorant in some way or other. We just look at the surface of things and can't understand the deeper meaning. For example, someone's personality, we judge it as bad or good, based on how they benefited us or how they acted in a short time. We ignore the fact that humans are so complex and are composed of so many layers and parts that there is no bad or good. Bad and good are behaviors, not the actual human. Talking to someone like you who approaches the situation with knowledge, therefore not judging it, just feels so comfortable and gives me a sense of relief. I don't think I have anyone to talk to. I mean, I have a lot of people around me, but they usually come to me for help, and I'm not used to asking anyone for help, or showing them that I have problems, too. Or, I feel like they have it much worse than I do, and why should I bother them with my problems? For example, a family member, who I don't consider happily married, called me and wanted to give me advice regarding my marriage. What she was saying was so far from what I wanted to hear, and her pattern of thinking was so different from mine, that I found myself feeling frustrated just listening to her.

After that, I decided to act assertively and tell them respectfully that I don't need to hear their advice, and if I need advice I'll ask whoever I feel can help me. I thought, these people just love giving advice and preaching. I wanted to tell them, "You should go work on your own many problems," but stopped myself. It's like they want to help you, not because they really want to help you, but because they want to give themselves credit that they did. I believe a real help is according to what the person you are intending to help really needs, not what you think is good for them. It seems like with my family, they want to help, but according to their definition of what helping is, and how they want to provide it, not what the person really needs. My definition of helping is according to the person's needs. If we don't know what they are, we should just stay out, because then whatever we do is a selfish act, not a helping hand. It seems to me that most people think they know a lot more than they really do.

Then came a quietness, and she continued:

Sara: My childhood, where do I start? I was the only girl among my brothers. My father was a businessman, who worked most of the time during my childhood. He had a lot of traditional ways of thinking. For example, he used to make what seemed to be a deal with God, that if God gave him sons, he would feed about fifteen poor people. When he got a daughter, he was okay with one, but didn't want any more. He was very open about this. I felt that I was very different from others in my childhood. For as long as I can remember, I had a deep sense of compassion for others, and wanted to give and get love more than others around me. For example, I remember spending my allowance money to buy poor children chocolate. I didn't even tell my mom, because she didn't approve of it. I mean, she had no problem helping the poor, but she didn't want me to spend my allowance on that. But it seemed that I had to do it. A force overcame me, which I could not control. Even as a child, I would get upset from anything that seemed to me like an injustice. For example, I had this neighbor girl who was treated differently because she was a Jew. I really liked this girl, and choose to be her best friend. This action caused my other friends to walk away from me, but I didn't care. I wanted to be with her, and found myself defending her every time others were making up stories about her.

Or, as another example, I would feel extremely affected by other people's suffering, especially those who had no control over the suffering they were going through. For example, a helpless child who was being abused would just make me overwhelmingly upset, and I wanted to do something about it. I also had this teacher side in me, and was able to attract others to listen to me and to form a group. In high school, I had my own group of girls who were considered the popular group. We would hang out and have fun.

During my childhood and growing up, my father and mother did not have a very healthy relationship. I actually don't remember any of my family members whom I considered as having a healthy relationship, but some of them were in harmony with each other. What I mean by this is that although the marriage didn't look healthy from outside, or from my perspective, they didn't fight about the problems they had. Now that I look back, I see that even though they looked unhappy to me, they might have been okay with each other because they were similar. Or, I should say, they were at the same level of understanding of what life is all about. I see now that when a couple is at a different level of understanding, they can really frustrate and upset each other, and block each other's growth, and especially that the one who is at a more limited level can damage the one at a higher level.

For example, among two people, if one is a first grader and one in middle school, they won't have a lot in common and will have a lot that they don't understand about each other. But if they're both first graders, they have much more things they can share. Does it make sense to you, what I am saying?

Therapist: I hear you. A good example I use to demonstrate this is having a married couple come into my office for marital difficulties. Sometimes, seeing the pattern is very easy, one is more under the control of her child side, and the other is the more mature one.

What's obvious in any type of relationship is that there are signs to let us know whether a relationship is unhealthy. When these signs are present, the worst thing we can do to ourselves is to just let them stay the way they are, without taking any action to either fix it or release it.

There's a point where we have to get from a point of wondering what to do and self-pity, to taking action. There are long-term consequences to negative relationships. Every relationship needs a reasonable level of stability and compatibility. Sometimes, the dynamic of the individual's interaction needs to change. In your diaries, I read the word "back-stabbing" a number of times. You feel like some family members back-stabbed you during your divorce, by the examples you provided, and that's a strong emotional feeling. You feel like they were not supportive, and acted in selfish ways. Yet, having this inner feeling and continuing to have a relationship with them as if nothing has happened would be very questionable. What you did was perhaps the best way to go. You decided, a number of times, to try to explain things to them. When you felt like it seemed like they just did not want to understand, you decided to stop talking to them until you were ready, or, I should say, until they were ready to understand that this is your life, and they have no right to make decisions for you, and that what they were doing was a selfish act rather than a helpful one.

If they are not able to comprehend this fact, then it's totally up to you as to how you want to react, whether you want to start a relationship with clear boundaries, to make sure they don't cross and disrespect your boundary, like before, or just decreasing the friction altogether and minimizing your communication with them. This is totally your choice, and no one has the right to tell you what to do. You go with your inner feelings, and your reasoning associated with the feelings.

What an emotionally healthy human would do is not let anyone cross her boundaries without her permission, and for her not to be treated like a valueless human who cannot make decisions for herself.

The same goes for every situation; a cheating/controlling husband, a parent who neglects her child, is in complete denial over it, and expresses complete surprise about the estranged relationship, a friend who has two faces, and a co-worker who lies. All these are example of bad relationships people may have. It's totally a personal decision about how one wants to deal with a "bad" relationship. For a person who wants to make it better, there are two ways. Either to take steps to change the dynamics of the relationship to make it better, or to move out of the relationship and get on with her life.

The fact that one has to pay attention to is that if one does not take any action and lets the unhealthy relationship be as it is, there are serious long-term consequences. Some examples would include a wearing away of self worth, or an unhealthy marriage where, suddenly, the only identity the person has is the one placed on her by her abuser, controller, or neglector. She sees herself through his eyes, not out of love and unity, but out of powerlessness and lack of control. This person may suffer from serious personality disorders.

Another damaging effect would be this person's inability to accept the love of another person and its good intentions. She becomes suspicious of other's sincerity, which leads to undermining the possibility of future positive relationships. This person, subconsciously, expects the same treatment from others, making it difficult for her to engage in a healthy relationship in which there is genuine love and acceptance.

A relationship is unhealthy if the person feels afraid of the other, feels controlled or unable to express true feelings and thoughts, feels happier when this person is not around, wants to get out but don't want to be lonely, feels small or inadequate, and feels neglected physically and emotionally. If one feels one of the above, it means that one is probably in a dysfunctional relationship and needs to make a decision as to what she wants to do, or whether she wants to continue with it. It might be time to do an evaluation of the benefits she gets from it versus the harm it imposes upon her. If the second outweighs the first, it's time to take some serious action for change.

Please note that I use she, but it can be a he as well. Does what I explained make sense, so far?

Sara: It makes great sense. I know of many women who don't have an identity. It's as if their identity is that of their husband. My belief is that if they were happy and at peace with that sense, then that would have been okay, but the ones I know are not happy. They have many physical and mental issues. Most of them are in total denial, and are being affected by it. They're suffering, but don't know what they're suffering from, and are living a very illusory life.

It's amazing how being aware of a situation makes one's perspective of it so very different. In my case, I was more aware, but it seemed to me that my ex-husband was in total sleep. His mood would change *totally* over small things, like a child that get overly sad or happy over a piece of candy. He was in *total denial* of everything. To this day, he still amazes me by how far from reality he really is, and what a deep sleep he's in. Maybe you can help me understand this more.

Therapist: That's right. Let me elaborate on the discussion of the relationship to clarify one thing. We discussed the child side and adult side. I'll use the following example, referring to the child side as the man, and the more adult side as the woman. When this couple came to the office and were asked what brought them in, the one who has his child side in control might say, "My marriage is great, I don't know what's wrong, she just complains about little things, I don't see any problems, I just came here because she asked me to." He might blame others for the problems, and never admit that he has any part in this.

His child side is not able to see he's a part of it. He just wants to have his basic needs met and move on. He does not comprehend her level of frustration, or what she's trying to communicate with him. He just doesn't get it, and it seems like he doesn't care. Even if he reports he gets it, it doesn't seem genuine. On the other hand, the woman who is more mature may feel frustrated, anxious, and overwhelmed, and can't wait to either fix what she sees as crushing problems or get out of the marriage. She feels like she's trapped and suffocating.

How I explain this is that the person who feels happy is like the child who is asking for candy, and as long as he has it, he's satisfied and unaware of how those around him feel. But the more mature person, feeling neglected and misunderstood because of living with a child, wants to fix the problem, only to feel more frustrated. This happens when the level of understanding between a couple is too different. Solving their problems can be very challenging, if not impossible. There is no harmony, and such a couple is unable to see eye to eye. In a relationship like this, compromises become hard, if not impossible. They just cannot happen naturally, like in a harmonious relationship.

Sara: That's so true. I feel like I was living with a child during my marriage. I truly do, except that it was a child who had contaminated intentions, not pure ones. You know how a child is innocent and makes mistakes, but without harmful intentions. With my husband, it seemed like he intentionally wanted to hurt me if he thought he didn't have control. He had some inner anger toward me for not feeling attracted toward him. Referring back to what I was saying, I see now that a couple does not have to meet my standards of a relationship. As long as they're similar in their pattern of thinking and behavior, then they're okay. During my childhood, we did have some happy and good times, but, at the same time, some sad times. Many people in my family seemed to pretend that they had a good life, but deep down they seemed unhappy and lost. I know you said you'd explain it later, but can you do it now?

Therapist: Sure. As I referred to it briefly before, in Jungian psychology this mask or pretend you're referring to is called a persona, meaning it's a mask people put on to hide their true being and feelings, because they're scared to face what's really there. Jung introduced the term shadow, which he identified as anything that's unconscious, repressed, undeveloped, and denied by the individual. We all have shadows, he said, and should understand what it is.

We can use this example of situations in which we were made uncomfortable by someone else's actions, or even presence. Whenever an action, quality, or characteristic in another person brings about strong emotional reactions in us, we can be sure that we're feeling a part of our own shadow. These qualities may be the exact opposite of what we think we may have. So, we have them, we're just not aware of them. On the other side of the story is a person who has a positive side of our shadow and will draw us toward herself or himself. This could be what's called the Gold part of our shadow. This is our psyche's way of bringing itself into our awareness and consciousness. It's a signal we should pay attention to. For example, when the first thing in a person that bothers us is how aggressively he acts, we might want to look at our own level of anger, or when we're attracted to someone through meeting them once, we might want to look at ourselves to see what inner qualities we share with them that attracted us to them. Is it clear so far?

Sara: Yes. Please tell me more. This is really interesting. And where does persona go in here?

Therapist: You used an example of people acting unreal, or, as you worded it, as them "pretending." We've all come across people we thought were acting "too nice," or "too happy." Something told you that this may not be their true self, or that in some ways they're acting fake when we're around them. These are the type of people who may be buried behind a mask of persona, which is a false portrayal of self. These types of people will intentionally avoid any type of negative emotion. By denying these parts of their selves, they will suppress them and make them denser and darker, while at the same time dragging themselves into a state of dishonesty to themselves and to others. Is it clear so far?

Sara: Yes, so what should we do about it?

Therapist: We should learn, recognize, and process our dark or shadow side to be able to control it. As Jung says, "Whatever one does not live, lives against one." We should be aware of the fact that if these parts are hidden within the unconscious, it doesn't mean they're not active in our life. They're very much active, but have control over us, rather than us having control over them. Now, when a person pretends to be something she is not, she will be dragged into believing her pretended self instead of her real self. This will cause her not to make a move for change and maturation according to her true sense of being.

For example, a person who denies she has anger issues can live under her anger's control. She many lose many opportunities in life due to that anger, without even knowing it. It can be a passive anger or an active anger. But, until she acknowledges this part of her shadow, she is unable to be in control of it.

Sara: I think I did that, too.

Therapist: What do you mean?

Sara: Well, sometimes I had a disguise on my self. At times, I pretended to be something I was not, and in the process I forgot who I truly was. I wanted to look like someone who had it all and had a perfect life. I wanted to look "ideal." Meanwhile, I think I had a lot of inner anger, because I felt I deserved to be happier.

Therapist: Can you give me an example that shows that disguise and how you felt?

Sara: For example, my marriage. Even thought it was damaging to me, I pretended that I had a good marriage. I never felt comfortable telling anyone in my family and/ or my friends about what was really going on. Or another example, I idealized my dad and the relationship I had with him, never truly thinking about how it was and what was going on. It seemed like I was in a deep sleep.

Therapist: That sense of feeling uncomfortable telling others, where do you think that came from? Did you think they'd judge you, or that they won't understand, or that, since they had their own problems to deal with, they weren't going to care or understand?

Sara: That's a good way of putting it. I think, it was a combination of all of them. I wanted to look ideal, if there is such a thing. I wanted to look like somebody who had it all. I wanted my parents to be proud of me for making it all work, especially my dad. I wanted to be better than others. I wanted to be everyone's role model.

Therapist: So that concept of being better than others, did it work, did it give you that feeling?

Sara: Um, not really. For a while, on the surface it might have, but deep down inside, it made me feel worse than it would have if I'd learned to be myself. I dealt with feelings of extreme anxiety, not knowing what they were. I thought it was normal to be anxious.

Therapist: So, if you had learned to expose your true self, then you think you would have been able to feel the joy of you being you, rather than trying to be something impossible, which is your ideal, untrue self. Did I get that right?

Sara: Exactly.

Therapist: The concept of being ideal or perfect, what

do you mean by that? I mean, where did you get that concept, because whatever pattern of thinking we have, we have it due to some period of our life and what has been injected into us. Who expected you to be ideal? Who gave you this pattern of irrational thinking that one could be ideal according to other people's expectations?

Sara: Well, I think part of it has to do with the fact that I was born into a family that valued boys more than girls, openly. Most of them did not value women that much. And the worst part is that the women believed that, and didn't seem to want to do anything to make a change for the better.

From the time I remember, I had to work harder and be different than what my being craved for, in order to be able to please my parents, especially my dad, who thought girls had to have a specific form of behavior, way of life, and thinking. I think I always shaped myself according to what he saw as a "good girl." I always had to prove myself, and that caused me some inner anxiety and anger, as well. I mean, I'm not an angry person, but I feel upset because of this unfair treatment. I was always so much more capable than my brothers, but always felt like I was viewed as less. Even now that I'm very successful and have many positive things going for me, it seems like my father is disappointed in me for the divorce. What do you think about that?

Therapist: Well, I think that's certainly unfair for you, to feel like you were viewed as less than your brothers, or that there were two sets of expectations. We all have a need to be loved by our parents and our family. It's supposed to be unconditional. But, unfortunately, too many times, for selfish reasons or for other people's ignorance, we don't get that feeling. Let me explain something before getting to this point, because it seems related here. We all have needs, which go from lower to higher levels, some of which we grow out of, according to our level of maturity. Lower forms of needs are things that are biological, like eating and shelter. Then comes a sense of security, etc. Higher needs are the needs for love, approval, and, if they go higher, they can go all the way to a deep sense of connection to something within that is superior to our personality and way of thinking, which some call a need for self-actualization, and then, afterward, a sense of connection to the bigger picture, which some may call spirituality. It seems like your need for approval to have a sense of security in life, which started in childhood, was still strongly functional within you when you grew up, and was causing you to block yourself from moving forward to fulfilling your higher needs. By that I mean, for example, wanting your dad's approval of who he thought was an ideal you, had made you make decisions that you did not want to make, but made anyway to make sure you kept that image of your dad's ideal girl, which by itself led to damaging your sense of true being, and resulted in blockages leading to anxiety and some form of inner anger or unhappy feelings. Am I on the right track so far?

Sara: Yes, yes, please go on.

Therapist: As humans, we can categorize ourselves into different levels of essence in order to be able to comprehend the process more clearly. There is a lower level of the self, which is called the child self by some. There is a more mature one that is called the adult self, and there is a wise one which we can call the guidance self.

Please pay attention to this important point, which I always try to emphasize, that these concepts and categorizations are the best we, at this point in psychology, are doing to put a label on something as complex as the human psych, in order to be able to clarify our points. It does not mean that the human psych is limited to these categorizations. It just means that we're trying to explain it in a way understandable to people. So, to go back to the subject, what happens most of the time is that even though we may be physically at an older age, we are, sometimes, still letting the child self be at work without any control and/ or guidance from the other two selves. In other words, the conscious or adult selves should become dominant and take charge of the child self, making choices for it and being aware of the consequences of each choice, to be able to see whether that choice is the right one. Is it clear so far?

Sara: Yes, so what do we do to get there?

Therapist: When we start the process of knowing ourselves, it means discovering and acknowledging these parts, which results in the conscious self becoming more aware of one's characteristics and eccentricities. It means realizing that every person is a unique individual, with different challenges, strengths, and weaknesses in life. We have to learn about all different parts of us, the ones we like and the ones we don't like, accept them, balance them, process them, and move on. Denying a part of us will come back to haunt us, one way or another. Working through and acknowledging these different parts of us, enables us to be able to understand and heal the wounds that caused the repression that is deep inside us. It enables us to become more of who we really are, moving toward the authentic personality. We don't want to repeat the unconscious patterns of behaviors that are unproductive. The more we move toward our real self, the more we have access to a greater depth of meaning in our everyday lives. When you came in the first day, you said that you wanted to learn to be self-actualized, and that's what you're trying to do with these therapy sessions. Some examples that Dr. Maslow might have used as self-actualized individuals are Abraham Lincoln (in his last years), Thomas Jefferson, Benjamin Franklin, George Washington, Albert Einstein, Aldous Huxley, William James, Spinoza, Goethe, Pablo Casals, Pierre Renoir, Robert Browning, Walt Whitman, Henry Wadsworth Longfellow, Eleanor Roosevelt, Jan Addams, Albert Schweitzer, Ralph Waldo Emerson and Franz Joseph Haydn, among many others. Some that I may add to this list, who have gone above the self-actualization process into the self-transcendence, would be people like Ghandi, Abu Ali Sina (Avecena), Rumi, Buddha, and the prophets. These are people who not only have not taken more than needed from life, but also have contributed greatly to this world before their passage from this world.

The attention-grabbing part is that these "role models" were also acknowledged by Dr. Bucke in his book, *Cosmic Consciousness,* as people who demonstrated the behavior of people who had experienced cosmic consciousness. This cosmic consciousness could be similar to what Carl Jung explains as the collective unconscious. Psychologists believe that there are about 2% of the population who can truly be identified as self-actualized and even fewer can go higher than that. A self-actualized person is a person who is realistically-oriented, and has a more efficient perception of life, is not scared of the unknown, has an expanded ability to reason and see the truth in a logical way, has self acceptance, and as a result more acceptance of what life brings about, does not suffer from too much guilt or shame, enjoys her time without regrets or apologies, is spontaneous, is simple in her inner life, has autonomous ethics, and seeks continual growth.

A self actualized person is focused on learning about the self. It's like a mission for her to improve her core self. She's detached from what is not needed or harmful to her, is a self starter, and can enjoy time with herself and live in privacy without being antisocial, lacks unnecessary worries, and is devoted to duty.

A self-actualized person also has an open mind rather than a stereotypical one, which leads her to appreciate things for their basic good in life. Other characteristics are autonomy, peak experiences, clear boundaries in a relationship, being aware, self disciplined, self assertive, knowing one's strengths and weaknesses, and accepting them and trying to improve them. These are some of the many characteristics, and that is what we're all craving for. Now, one can go even higher than that, to a total transformation. Are you sensing what I'm communicating?

Sara: Definitely. I really want to find a meaning in my life. This is what I want to become; self-actualized in its true sense. I want to see where I belong. I want to find myself. I want to see what makes me happy in its true sense. I want to let go of my rootless guilt, anxiety, sadness, and all the negative feelings that are so intense. When I look around me and see people living a very shallow life, I feel such compassion for them, but at the same time want to make sure I don't live like that. I want to let go of being mad and blaming those who caused me to be unhappy, and any negative emotion that is harmful to me and my mental/coral health. Can you explain this term, self-actualization, a little more?

Therapist: Okay. As we said, through this therapy process, one of our goals will be to walk you through the process of self-actualization. Self-Actualization is on the top of the human hierarchy of needs, right before self-transcendent.

Dr. Maslow was the one who referred to it first. He summarized the concept as: "A musician must make music, an artist must paint, a poet must write, if he is to be at peace with himself. What a man can be, he must be. This is the need we may call self-actualization ... It refers to man's desire for fulfillment, namely to the tendency for him to become in actuality what he is potentially: to become everything that one is capable of becoming ..."

You also referred to happy and unhappy feelings. Let me give a brief explanation of that, and then go back to something else. Many people come to me from all areas of life; physicians, researchers, teachers, housewives, politicians, etc., and ask me what the definition of happiness is. There seems to be trouble with people sustaining their happiness. They try so hard to get something to feel happy, and then after a short while that feeling seems to be fading away, only to find themselves looking for more. It seems so limitless and a never-ending story, this search for happiness. They never stop to think what it really means to be happy. Is it according to other people's definition, or according to one's own unique needs and personality?

One reason for this may be that we don't know what

happiness is, or that it may be a very personal experience, depending on who you are, where you belong on the pyramid of growth, and how much you want from life. Happiness is related more to the expansion of our view of life, rather than what we have and hold. Pursuit of happiness is a life-long goal, and one needs to learn about herself and the techniques of mental state needed to achieve it. A lack of inner development is the cause of imbalance in the person, causing unhappiness and dissatisfaction in life.

We have to start with cleaning up our mental environment from any harmful elements, so that our true sense of happiness can resurface, the one we had as children. In many technologically advanced countries, people try to achieve this happiness through materialistic forms. Advertisements try to make them believe they need something to be happy, but they get that thing only to find out it was a very temporary and shallow happiness. Then another and another, a seemingly endless story, sometimes, they put too much burden on themselves to get that temporary feeling, only to be disappointed later on. Too many times, they look back and wish they hadn't made "those" choices, since the cost outweighed the benefit, either in physical and emotional cost or spiritual cost. Even those who know that this does not bring happiness, and have reached that conclusion, do not see another way. They withdraw into their comfort zone, fencing themselves off from what seems to them as a hostile and threatening world. Some of us spend a lifetime attaining and protecting in pursuit of happiness, but never truly feel it for more than a short period at a time, in its real sense.

A true definition of happiness would be a life with healthy connections rather than damaging attachments, being able to accept what is pleasant without clutching, and being able to accept the unpleasant when we have to, without condemning with negative emotions for long. It has been shown that the ways we look for happiness often prevent us from finding it, in reality. I will point to the concept of happiness more during the course of these sessions, but for now, since you mentioned this word, I thought it relevant to point to it, briefly. Now, you were talking about your father, I want to hear more about that. Tell me about your childhood home environment and your parents' relationship. Did you feel like you had a safe home while growing up?

Sara: A safe home? You know, I've thought about this for such a long time. What's amazing is that up to a few months ago, I thought I had a wonderful childhood. But the more I think about it, and the more I get out of that denial stage, the more I see the negative sides of my childhood. My childhood was a combination of things. Now, I'm starting to think, if I deny them and they're still there, what are they doing to me? As you said, by denying them, I'm not making them go away, they're very much active in me, but by denying them, they're in control of me, not me in control of them. That may be the cause of some of my emotional pain. Right?

Therapist: That's right. By denying your suppressed memories, and by not acknowledging your different parts and different experiences of life, you, in a way, let them work at their own pace and let them be in charge of your thoughts and actions, rather than you having control over them. Okay, our time is running out, and we will not be able to start your childhood memories now, because of the time limit, but we'll discuss it during the next sessions. In the meantime, I want you to start reading this article in your free time. Let me know how it went. Many concepts in it are similar to what we talk about in therapy. Any questions or anything else you wanted to add before we end today's session?

Sara: This is so fascinating. Time flew by. No, no questions for now. So how many pages of this should I read?

Therapist: It's up to you. Go at your own pace and need. There are no "shoulds." There is guidance, with freedom.

At the end of each session, Sara was given a relaxation phase, asked how she felt about the session, and given some form of homework to do. In this homework, she was encouraged to monitor her thinking pattern closely, and to be aware of where each intense thought came from. Sometimes, clients don't feel comfortable with the homework at first, but find it rewarding after getting used to it. These homework assignments help clients visualize their emotional state by writing it down, which can help them with focusing on the issues or seeing their thinking patterns that waste a lot of their energy. This can be followed by replacing these dysfunctional patterns of thinking, which have possibly been imitated from generation to generation, to a more evolved form of thinking that matches a healthy lifestyle for them.

Session 2

The following session, Sara came in looking very eager to start the process. The therapist asked her about her week and chatted with her a little bit.

> **Sara:** My week was a combination of everything. It seems like my eye is opening up. I felt joy, sadness, anger, excitement, happiness, and some other feelings, but more intensely than I've ever felt before. It was like I was more aware of my feelings, and accepted them, and was looking for a reason for why they were there. I felt lonely, at times. I don't know how to explain it. It was a feeling like the one you explained, surrounded by people, yet feeling alone. I've also started enjoying time with myself more than before. I spend hours with myself without being bored. My writing has become something of a miracle. I sit for hours and write; it just comes. It's like therapy. I want to find my path in life, and feel like I've found an open door with an invitation to enter. In a way, the door was always there, but I'm noticing it now. One that really does belong to me, one that comes from

my true state of being and my own passion, rather than what others think is good for me and what will impress others. I tried for years to impress others, and look what happened. I ended up being anxious and feeling like I blocked myself from many real talents that I had. I used to be a good drawer, a good writer, and many other talents. but I never pursued them until my divorce time came. As soon as my husband moved out, that sense of talent, all of a sudden, nourished in me and I started to draw magnificent pictures, write poems, and write my first real book.

Therapist: Oh, that's so amazing! I would love to see some of your work, as soon as you feel like they are ready. What do you mostly write about?

Sara: Mostly personality, nature, one's essence, and love. This is one of many examples. Do you want to hear one of my poems?

Therapist: Sure.

Sara: This came when I discussed aggressiveness vs. assertiveness. I do believe we have to respect others as much as we respect ourselves, but we also have to learn to be assertive. Assertiveness is a way to not let others take advantage of us. I also talk about the importance of learning healthy ways to defend oneself when we're being attacked by an emotional intruder. Some people seem to enjoy crossing other people's boundaries for no specific reason. They just do it to get more materialistic satisfaction, or some form of instant gratification, because they are still, somehow, unfulfilled of their childhood needs. I do believe that every human being has a right to defend her or himself from harm. For example, myself, I try not to bother anyone and live a productive life, but when my ex-husband was trying to harm me, I defended myself the best way I could, but I was in a position of defending, not attacking. I just wanted him to get off my back and leave me alone. Well, let me not get off track. Here's what I wrote:

"I asked the bee, why do you strike?

"To protect.

"I asked the snake, why do you harm?

"To feel less threatened by them coming too close.

"I asked the lion, why do you attack?

"To protect my territory.

"I asked the bird, why do you attack?

"To protect my children.

"All the animals seemed to have a reason for their survival, whether or not it was obvious to my five senses.

"I asked humans, why do you harm, attack, molest, assail, damage, harass, bother, assault, and hurt?

"Because I am greedy, power-thirsty, self-centered, ignorant, inconsiderate, boorish, and unaware.

"I felt sad and speechless.

"So you are even lower than these animals

"They seem to be attacking for survival but you...

"They were not ready to hear what I had to say,

"So I walked away with sorrow."

Therapist: That was very meaningful. Writing is a great way of self-expression. I would be happy any time you feel like sharing one of these with me. So your week has been a week full of a combination of experiences. Tell me about your peak experience.

Sara: My peak experience, um. … I think it was this past Friday night. I put on some relaxing music and started reading a book. Going through the first and the second chapters, reading those beautiful poems, and relating them to myself, and then to the explanation I was getting through these poems. I felt that I was Rumi, the poet I was reading; I experienced his words. It gave me chills. It seemed like I was apologizing to the different parts of my self for ignoring them. I promised myself that I would take care of me, and find my inner balance and my inner peace. It seemed like I had a sense of shame for being superficial and shallow, sometimes, despite the fact that every part of my being and psych were seeking a meaning in life.

Since I was a teenager, I was seeking this meaning. I went to spiritual classes in search of meaning, but was never satisfied with them. They were all missing something, in my eyes. They just didn't provide what I was looking for. My peak experience of this week would be the bliss I felt that night. I've started feeling that more often now than before. I don't need to do much to sense that blissfulness. It usually comes when I'm deep down into my silence. I guess you can call it meditating. I can't quite explain it with words.

Therapist: And what was it that you were looking for during that phase of meditation?

Sara: I wanted to know, I wanted to learn about my purpose in life, and the meaning of life in general. I couldn't go on denying or avoiding it, I didn't want to go on living my life superficially and wasting it. I didn't want to believe something I was told without thinking about it, deeply. I was searching for a way based on reason, not on repetition of words. I wanted to listen to someone whose intention was not to make money or gain power or attention, but to truly just tell the truth. Someone who could connect with my inner core being, someone I could trust. Someone who talked based on knowledge, and was aware of science and facts.

I was looking for that someone within myself.

I wanted to find the meaning of my life, my intention, my passions, and my inner balance. I wanted to find the roots of why I was so anxious; why I would go so far trying to look a certain way, while feeling different inside. Somehow, I had gotten far away from my core. I had anxiety because of the unhappiness I was experiencing. It seemed like I was pushing myself to enjoy things that others were enjoying, but it was like a mocking action. It wasn't giving me a sense of joy. What made me really happy was helping others in a truly useful sense and being with people I enjoyed, but many times the people I spent time with weren't in harmony with me, and sometimes I ended up loosing my true sense of who I am to try to be a part of what they were doing; to connect with them, I guess. I don't know how to explain it. Can you tell me why I was doing that? I really want to hear it from your point of explanation.

Therapist: Well, it could have many reasons. One that

comes to mind would be when a person feels incomplete or insecure because of her lack of knowledge of herself. This is a person who does not value herself as she is, or, in other words, a person who does not trust herself, not because she isn't good enough, but because she hasn't been able to see her true goodness. This person tries to be like others, to fit in and to be liked by others, even if it means being untruthful to herself. This person may turn into a people-pleaser, wanting to keep everyone happy at the cost of her own emotional well-being. For example, she does things without thinking whether she likes them or not, whether they're beneficial to her mental health and balance, or, even if there is a point in doing them, she does it because others are doing it, or because she wants to be liked by others, or some other reason. Now, let's go back to your childhood story to see where this is rooted. Knowing where the root is will help us understand it better, and understanding it will help in the process of healing. Tell me about your relationship with your mom and dad and your brothers.

Sara: As I said before, my mom and dad did not have the healthiest relationship. They did not live in harmony. They were so much the opposite of one another. My mom was more educated than my dad, and that, among other things, caused a lot of problems. I remember them acting very cold towards each other, especially my mom toward my dad. A woman's kindness toward her husband was missing in my mom. I remember some forms of abuse, regular arguments and yelling. I remember, my mom being cold toward me during most of my childhood, maybe because she thought I was taking my dad's side. I remember what I sensed as my mom being jealous of me when my dad showed me attention and love. I didn't know it was jealousy back then, but she acted very cold, and sometimes even mean to me. I always tried very hard to get the love I wasn't able to get from my mom through my dad, and my dad's side of the family.

I think my mom was depressed. She seemed controlling, cold, and just didn't show me any form of love. She loved to preach and tell me and others what to do. There was a teacher in her that just didn't have a limit. Even now, every chance she gets, she wants to give me advice, and, of course, I don't agree with her advice most of the time and have told her many times that I don't need to hear that from her, but she keeps on doing it anyhow. I feel like she has no respect for me. She just does what she feels like she needs to do, and then she gives herself credit for being caring about me and wanting to tell me what to do.

I always tell her, "But mom, that's not being caring! You would be caring if you give me what I really need, not what you think I need."

During my childhood, I specifically remember an incident in which a friend of mine's mom kissed her when we went to her house for play time, I envied that so much. I wished I had a mom who would kiss me and love me and show me kindness, but I never felt that I got that.

I know my mom loved me. She cared about my school and my education, up to the point that she could. But, somehow, I remember more negative memories with her than positive. Many days, I was left alone, even during my younger years, as young as elementary school, I felt very scared, since we had a big house. I remember many times I was verbally abused for making typical mistakes. I felt very lonely as a child, and was constantly trying to get love and attention from others, and in many ways was successful in doing so. I was always popular in my school, among my friends, and with my family. I was usually the center of attention, and people enjoyed my company, but at what cost? I specifically tried very hard to please my dad. I remember being hit a lot by my older brother, and I remember my mom not doing anything to defend me. She would just watch it. Or she would even cause the fight by complaining about me to my brother. She had a habit of doing that. Oh my God, why is it all bad memories in my head? I know I had some good ones, but it seems like I can't think of any of them. I need to take a breath. Can I have a cup of water?

Therapist: Sure. While I get you a cup of water, listen to this soothing music. Relax and calm your mind, imagine each part of your body relaxing, and just be in the moment. The tape will guide you...

I went back to give her some time by herself. When I returned, she seemed to have cried, but seemed more relaxed. At times, she becomes overwhelmed by her memories. This is typical in patients who have repressed their memories for so long, and denied that they exist. When and if, at a point in their life, they decide to make a change and to start the process of healing, acknowledging and processing these suppressed and concealed memories is very difficult at first, but rewarding afterward, and is very much needed for the true healing process.

Therapist: How do you feel?

Sara: Okay, I guess.

Therapist: Whenever you're ready, we can continue with that, but I want you to tell me a couple of your joyful memories before you go on with your previous conversation. The reason is that I feel you're overwhelmed by these recollections, and I want you to feel a sense of balance.

Sara: You know doctor, I need to be free. I want to feel free. I read about self- liberation, and learned a lot about it. I wish I could be that. Can we talk about it a little bit before I talk about my childhood experience? What is this liberation? I don't know of anyone in my family or friends who seems to have gotten there. I don't know if I will ever be able to be completely free. I think that this is the type of experience that self-actualized people will have.

Therapist: Sure, we can discuss that. As I told you in the first session, my approach to your case will be eclectic or multimodal, with a focus on self-psychology. So, I'll go with your needs. You have to be aware of the stages of becoming aware of suppressed memories, especially the unpleasant ones, in order to be able to process and go through each of them in a reasonable and healthy manner. None of these stages are abnormal. They're all normal parts of experience, as long as the person is aware of them and is working on passing through them and not getting stuck in one stage. Once an unpleasant suppressed memory comes out, the person passes through four main stages. Remember, I use the word main, because there are minor stages as well.

The first stage is denial, and then comes anger, depression, and acceptance.

Denial is when the person denies anything is wrong. An abused child who, as an adult, insists that they had perfect parents and a perfect childhood may be in denial. After becoming aware, the person can get out of the denial stage. This person may become angry at the situation, or the people surrounding the situation, that brought about the unpleasant memory or took something from this person. After that feeling is processed, a stage of sadness overcomes the person. After that, if all the stages are acknowledged and passed though with awareness, the last stage, which is the acceptance, will come to the person. If that makes sense, and you have no questions about it, we can move to your question.

Sara: Sure.

Therapist: So now let's discuss liberation. When it comes to the concept of liberation, many times we have to learn about how to let go of our attachments and unhealthy desires. Attachments could cause unhealthy connections and relationships in which someone will be harmed or blocked, because one can not let go when one should.

We have three types of adult relationships: Secure, avoidant, and anxious/ambivalent.

Secure adults are those who have a sense of healthy connection and have an easier time getting closer to others, and feel more comfortable when others get close to them. They don't worry about being abandoned, and have an easier time letting go of a relationship that isn't functional.

Avoidant adults are those who are uncomfortable being close to others, trusting others, and getting intimate. An example of this is a person who isn't able to show any kind of affection and love to his or her loved ones. And finally, the anxious adults find that others are unwilling to get as close as they would like them to, often worry that their significant other doesn't really love them, and want to merge completely with the other person, which sometimes can scare them away. This could be a controlling husband who wants his wife to be with him all the time, not letting her get out of his sight except in places where he's comfortable, with no rationality to it.

From what you've been explaining, in some forms of your relationships, but not others, you may have had some of the anxious adult in you. You may have wanted to get too close, too fast, and are scared of the concept of rejection. You're trying not to ever be rejected, even if that means pleasing others at the cost of your own emotional/ focal well-being. It also seems like your definition of a functional relationship may have been a poor definition before, but that you're getting closer to its true definition. It seems like you've come a long way from that, but should still be aware of it. How does that sound so far?

Sara: Please tell me more.

Therapist: So, based on what we talked about regarding different categories, the first category seems to be a much healthier form of attachment, which is referred to as a connection rather than an attachment. A healthy sense of connection can create a sense of freedom and love for the parties involved; one in which no one feels controlled, and compromises are made out of love and passion, not fear.

Many times, we mix up negative forms of attachment with love. For example, a mother who is insecurely attached to her child, constantly controlling and criticizing her, overly protecting her when she needs to let go, and feeling tired and overwhelmed when she needs to pay attention to her. Or it may be a husband who is anxiously attached to his wife, who develops obsessions and controlling and sometimes abusive behaviors with her. Or, it might be a friend with unreasonable expectations, who sees every action as a very personal matter, rather than seeing it from the other person's perspective.

All of us humans are craving a sense of connection to others, to our real self, to nature, etc. But many of us don't know how to do it, because we don't know who we are, what our roles are, and where we're heading. We, as humans, are supposed to be evolving emotionally and spiritually. By evolving I don't necessary mean we are from monkeys; by evolving I mean expanding, becoming more advanced, and making progress. We don't bond with others like Stone Age humans did, we bond based on how emotionally and spiritually close we feel to others. So, it's not always a family or blood-related bond, but is based on quality, not quantity. However, many of us have not emotionally, mentally, and spiritually evolved. We're stuck at earlier stages, and function from that level. Also, many of us don't know what love really means. We confuse love with anxious and insecure attachments. So, again, the first step will be finding our real self, a self without imposed irrational thinking patterns, a self who is working toward healing her damaged parts rather than denying they exist, a self who is what she was intended to be when she came to this world, but other factors in life changed it into something else that caused her to feel lost and confused. This lost sense of self will bring about a person who seems unable to differentiate different situations, actions, and consequences, who bases her life on what others think, and a pattern of unreasonable thinking that keeps on damaging her over and over again.

Now, our session is about over. I need you to relax and

tell me what you think while you take this paper home to fill out and bring it back for me. On this sheet of paper, I need you to tell me what you mean when you said, "I want to be completely free from these." What do you mean by the word, "these"? And tell me a little about your anxiety, when do you feel it most, what happens when you feel this, what goes through your mind, and whether there's anything you do to calm it down. Bring these for the next session. Any questions?

Sara: No, not really.

Therapist: How do you feel?

Sara: It was really good. I have to take it home and sleep on it, and do some work on it this week.

Therapist: Just remember, the process of healing, self-knowledge, and unfolding the layers of self is a process that needs focus and concentration, as well as commitment. It's like an onion; you peel off one layer and there comes another one. And you don't know when you'll get to the end, but it will become a part of you.

Sara: Thank you for everything...

Session 3

At the third session, Sara came in more relaxed. She had done the work I asked her to. This is typical of a client who is serious about self-knowledge, and these types of individuals have very good results because of their commitment to the process. I could see that Sara was a great candidate for going toward the process of self-growth. Sara was a very high-functioning client, who was not suffering from any form of disorder, but wanted to get help from a professional to resolve blockages she was not aware of. In other words, getting a second perspective from someone who would observe her rather than judge her, and would use knowledge to educate her about the part of herself she was not still in tune with. Not that many people are able to get all the way up here, not because they are not capable of it, but because they occupy themselves too much with the basic needs of life rather than going up the ladder of self-growth. Many others are in such a state of denial, avoidance, and suppression that they may never get to a point of feeling the need for a change and growth.

> **Therapist:** I see that you've done your work. How was it?

Sara: At first, I thought it was going to be strange, but it ended up being a good experience. I decided to put my doubts aside and trust the process. Every time I let my troubling thought processes come to me, they start engulfing me and interfering with the process I'm in. Writing about my anxiety made me become more aware of it. I see too many people who are so deep into their denial that you can't even tell them that there's another route. They would be self-defended; the deeper they're into this, the more the defense.

I was there, myself. I was one of those, if someone was to tell me, "Your anxiety may be coming from your childhood fears," I would respond, in an aggressive way, "What do you mean? I had a perfect childhood."

I would idealize everything, and the more I did, the more anxious I would become. I was truly ignorant when it came to self-knowledge and my emotionally/focal wellbeing. I was living a life of being untrue to myself.

Now, the more I dig in, the more I see it as it really was, the less defensive I become, and the more I'm ready to kiss a guiding hand. I see the fears I faced during my childhood, I see some of the abuse, both physical and emotional. I see the coldness, and my craving for love and attention. I see the unrealistic expectations put upon me as a girl. I see the sense of helplessness I experienced, and I see how this affected my life, because I was still living it. I'm also aware that I had a great number of blessings as a child, but it seems like my focus is more on the negative parts, for now. I think, when you were discussing the stages, I'm more in the stage of anger, for now. I've passed the denial stage and am in anger. But, hopefully, I will pass thought this and the sadness, and will come to accept things as they were, and move on.

I didn't take the initiative to step out of the zone I was in. As an adult, I don't have to live a life I don't like. I have choices. I have the power to change whatever I didn't like about my childhood upbringing, but it took me years to realize that. Again, it had become my comfort zone; a damaging comfort zone in which I wasn't growing, I was just living. I wasn't really being who I was supposed to be, who I came into this world to be, and who my true being was.

Life is an amazing, yet simple, process. The design is implemented in everything, simple and complex, two opposites at the same time. There are these sets of design structures we have to learn about, to apply them to ourselves to grow; otherwise life will block us.

Sometimes, when I'm ready, I will take myself back to my childhood. I imagine some of the bad memories. There are a few that really stick to my mind. One is the worst hitting I took from my dad. The hitting was so bad I wet myself. I was about 10 years old, and me and my brother got into a huge fight. My brother was always picking on me. He had this issue with his height and was picked on in school. He had no way to deal with that, so it turned into this inner anger that he would release upon me. He was about 10 years older. My mom witnessed this, but never did anything to stop it. She's still in her own denial. She thinks she was a great mother, and isn't ready to hear anything negative, so I don't even try. My relationship with her is not that close, but we talk and hang out every once in a while. That's enough for me, for now.

Anyway, my brother started hitting me. My dad walked in, couldn't catch my brother, so he started to hit me. I could feel he'd had a bad day. He really released it on me. He punched me, kicked me, slapped me, and just would not stop. I felt like I was dying. I felt like a worthless piece of meat. I felt so small, so "nothing." It got so bad and went on so long that my mother interfered, but even she couldn't stop him.

I am not sure, but I think I took about ten minutes of hitting, dragged myself to my room, and stayed there for the whole night. No one came to check on me. I don't remember what was going on in my mind. I don't remember any feelings I was experiencing. I think I just shut down, because I just didn't care anymore. Abuse was not a regular thing with my dad. I can remember him hitting me a few times, so it wasn't a regular thing, but even that was very painful, because there was no reason for it. It was unpredictable, and according to his mood.

I remember a couple of other incidents. I try to go to my childhood and place myself at the scene. I take myself to that lonely time after the abuse, I feel the feeling, and nurture my self and give my self hope and love. The more I do that, the more I feel this sense of liberation. At first it was really hard, but coming to you, and writing and talking about all these different aspects, made me get ready for it. I felt all these emotions of anger, hate, and resentfulness, but then they were replaced with an empty feeling. For a while, I felt nothing toward my mom and dad. Now, I feel like I'm stepping into the stage of acceptance; a true sense of forgiveness from within. I don't feel any negative feelings towards them anymore. I know they did the best they could, at the time.

I also know that, compared to other family members, I had the most and was the luckiest, especially when it came to material needs. I know that if my parents had the tools and opportunities to learn and get educated about raising a child, they would have followed it. It's just that they simply did not know. That's not an excuse. That's a reason that makes it easier for me to forgive and move on.

Now, I see it more as it really is. This helps with having a reasonable relationship with them. I do what makes me feel comfortable and avoid whatever I feel uncomfortable with.

I don't take in any form of guilty feeling that others try to impose upon me to make me do what they want me to. I do what I think is the right thing, not what others think. After all, most everyone else is so buried into their own set of denials or their own personal problems. How can they tell me what's right for me? Another thing that my writing, not just the writing itself but spending the time to think about my past, has taught me, is that it seems to me that I did, and in some ways still do, care a great deal about what others think, because I don't completely trust myself. I still feel insecure in some ways, and most of my anxiety comes from that.

For example, a lot of my thinking goes through what my ex-husband would do to me, what kind of stories he would make up about me, how he would try to damage me now, and all sorts of things related to him. How the fact that he is such a pathological liar and a story-maker will affect me and my children. How will his acting like an impulsive child who would do anything to hurt me, even using his own children, affect me and my children? Would he be able to damage my reputation in any way?

They say it takes years to build, but one mistake to destroy.

I know that he and his family are masters of making false accusations about others. I've seen them do it to others so many times. It's very easy for them to make horrific accusations against people. They don't have a clear conscience, and sometime they believe their own false accusations.

When I look at all these stressful thoughts that go through my mind, many of them I can control by not focusing on them, but some stick to me and bother me. If I separate from these patterns of thinking, and just release my self from reacting to them, then this individual will stop using them to frustrate me. All of these are in my mind. No one really believes him, and I have such a good reputation in my community that it takes a lot more than him to be able to destroy it. It seems like my ex-husband is very mad and has a lot of inner anger toward me. He is very much a passive-aggressive person. His anger does not seem to be because of something I did, but rather something I didn't do. He doesn't have the same passive wife, who would do anything to keep her marriage together and willingly continued to suffer. He feels not in control, and that's the reason he's mad.

I read about passive aggressiveness, and it describes him very well. He was one of those people who would behave and say one thing in your face, but do the opposite behind your back. He would hurt you, but indirectly. His mother was exactly the same way. She would behave nicest toward the people she hated

Most, and the list of people she hated goes on and on; basically anyone who had something positive going on for her or his life would be on her list.

Now that I went for the process of divorce, my ex-husband doesn't believe that he can control me anymore, so he's doing anything he can to get that sense of control back. He used my family, my friends, my money, making false accusations against me to destroy my reputation. You name it, he did it. He even used our children as a tool to try to frustrate me.

I've started to not react to his actions, one after the other, but still haven't been totally successful with two things:

one, my children, and the second, him making up stories about me. I'm getting better with the second, but am not sure I can ever be okay with the first. It just really bothers me when I feel like he may be using them as tools, or see them as his property. I spend every minute of my waking life thinking about how I can make it great for my kids. I go the distance to make sure I'm raising them in a very healthy environment. People who see them are very impressed by them, and I did it all by myself. My ex-husband didn't do anything to help. I feel like I spend a lot of time undoing his damage, rather than him helping me with the building process. You know?

Therapist: Sure. Let's go back to what you said about the two things your ex might be able to get on your nerves with, your children, and him making up stories about you, since you think he's a pathological liar. First one is your children. It seems, based on your diary and what we've talked about, that they're safe with him, physically. It's the emotional part that you're worried about. We'll get back to this.

Now, what do you think might happen if he does make up stories about you, or falsely accuse you? Let's get to the worse case scenario and move up to see what these accusations may do to you. Because, as the saying goes, they don't give sweets in a divorce, and that applies to many divorces. Usually, in a divorce, one wants it and the other is resistant towards it. Divorce should be one of many solutions to an unhealthy relationship, a way to free oneself if one feels s/he is not feeling nourished by the relationship. But, unfortunately, due to many people's sense of control, insecure attachments, and irrational patterns of thinking, one party or both may turn it into a war that one usually starts, but the other has to defend herself and fight back. There are not that many people who handle divorce very maturely. One always feels angry and mad at the other, while the other may feel a sense of relief. In your case, it seems like you're the one who senses this relief, but that your husband is reacting very harshly to the freedom you're experiencing. A lot is probably going through his mind, mostly coming from his emotional side. I don't really know your husband, but as time goes on and you give me more factual information, based on examples and incidents that happened, I'll be able to come up with a clearer picture of what may be happening to help you deal with it more reasonably and in a way that is the least damaging to your sense of self. Now, let's go back to the question I asked, what will happen if he makes false accusations?

Sara: I don't know, but some people may believe him. There are enough ignorant people out there who are ready to project their own issues on others, so they may believe anything he says without giving it a second thought. It's very easy to see through my ex-husband's lies, but there are enough ignorant people in the world to take what he says, repeat it to others, and spread a rumor.

It's amazing how some people are unreasonable and can damage you by their way of believing and behaving. Most everyone who really knows me didn't buy my ex's stories for even one second. Even though I'm a very private person and do not, at all, talk about my personal life to anyone, even my close friends, most of my close friends seem to think that my divorce had to automatically be my ex-husband's mismatch with me. I don't want anyone to think that it was anyone's fault, but people seem to want to find someone who is at fault. I think our marriage was just a bond in disharmony, and he might marry someone else who is in harmony with him and be happy. The same with me, even though, at this point, the *last* thing I'm thinking about is to get into a serious romantic relationship. I don't know. I might change my mind in the near future, but now I'm just not ready for it.

So, to return to your question, I don't know what will happen if he makes false accusations. He probably will, because he does it to everyone. It seems like gossiping about others is very normal in my ex's family. I'm sure my ex will continue this pattern, because if they do it to people close to them, what assurance do I have that they won't do it to me? After all, to them, now I'm the enemy, because I'm getting a divorce. People who truly know me make fun of him and his accusations, but what about those who don't know me?

Therapist: Why would you be concerned about those who don't know you? What you say may be true, and he may make up stories, especially since, according to your explanation, he loves it when he gets some form of attention by looking like the victim. What you need to realize is that when you want something to go away, you have to shift your focus away from, it both negatively and positively. If he gets a reaction from you, positive or negative, he will do it more. All he wants, at this point, is to get a reaction from you, to frustrate you, to trigger you, and to get under your skin. If you respond, he will do it more. If you ignore him, he will repeat it a couple of times and gives up.

Don't worry about what people might think. There are more than 5 billion of them in the world, and those who really know you would not believe anything peculiar he says, not even for one second. And the ones who don't know you, why should you even worry or care about what they think about you? As a person who is walking through self-actualization, this is one of the things we will work on. Once you start trusting yourself more, that fear will go away.

Now, this is something I would like you to think about more during this week and bring it to our next session. Time is running out and I want to review this week's work with you. I will review your last week's work, and will discuss it next time, as well.

At this point, Sara and I discussed extending the appointment time.

Therapist: For this week, I would like you to write for me of examples of your ex-husband's reaction toward your children, or his false accusations or talking about your private life to others, as I read in your diary, that may make you feel like an intruder is crossing your boundaries, and is discussing your private life with others without having any right to do so, or other negative behaviors that he imposed upon you that may have had some damaging effects on you. What goes through your mind, how do you react, and what you do to calm yourself down? ...

Session 4

At the next session, Sara came in with her homework. I had reviewed her previous work, and was ready to discuss it with her. She came in with a joyful face, like she always did. She looked well groomed and ready to start the process.

> **Therapist:** I went through your last homework. It seems like you have a lot of what you call the "peaceful time," and feel joy and bliss with your life. It seems like you think that if your ex-husband just leaves you alone and stops bothering you, then you'll feel very happy with your life. You wrote on three different places in your notes that, "There is no one I want to be, I'm so happy just being me and can't imagine being anyone else, I love my life with all its ups and downs."
>
> This is very good. You have a sense of satisfaction with your life, though you're aware of all its different elements. Many feel happy with their life, but are in a state of denial, can't move forward with it, and get stuck at one stage. You're well into the process of self-knowledge, and

are moving toward your destination. You seem to be more accepting of your life, and also more aware. Also, it seems like many of the anxiety symptoms you experience and many of the stress-related feelings are related to three categories; your children, your family's reaction to your divorce, especially the male figures, and your ex-husband's behavior. It seems like your children are the source of the most anxiety, because of your ex-husband's behavior towards them, and the fact that you're scared for their emotional wellbeing when they're with your ex-husband. Am I right so far?

Sara: Yes. I feel like my ex-husband wants to use them as tools to aggravate me. He doesn't know what love is. He looks at them as his property, and since his ego is feeling threatened by them not liking him, he wants to get back at them and me. He blames me for our children not liking him. He always blames others for his problems. Why is that?

Therapist: Well, we'll get back to that a little later. I want to finish reviewing this homework, because I want to make sure I got it right. We have to work on these, step by step, helping you feel more relaxed. It seems like you've been able to make many sudden changes, which is a result of your awareness. You've started to work on your well-being seriously, and I got that from your home work. Your pattern of thinking, and the behaviors that result from it, are much more improved over what they used to be. But, at the same time, with that change there are many new situations, some of which may look a little scary to you. It's normal in any circumstances where there is a change. There's an adjustment phase that comes with it. This adjustment phase may bring many challenges, but with a strong mind and determination, one would be able to pass through this adjustment phase.

What's still apparent is that there are still some of those irrational patterns in your thoughts. For example, what if people believe my ex-husband's stories, what if he destroys my reputation, what if he damages my boys' identity, what if I lose everything through this divorce, since he has the money and the ability to hire a powerful lawyer, and I have no money to do such a thing? All these "What ifs" are mingling your mind's pieces together. Now, tell me what if those things happen? What would happen? Let's go with the worst case scenario.

Sara: Well, I've tried so hard to get to where I am today. And, as the saying goes, it only takes one idiot to destroy what you have built for so long. Now, unfortunately, I have the idiot in my life. It is not hard to spread gossip.

Therapist: But who will believe the gossip? Think about it. Only those who feel insecure within themselves and feel lost. So, in reality, gossip is not the person who the gossip is about, but the people who listen and are attracted to it. Those are the type of people who do a lot of what psychologists call projection. Projection is one of the explanations for your question about why your ex-husband blames everyone but himself. When it comes to gossip, people project their inner hurt to escape the feeling of pain. Those are the buyers of gossip. And the path you're taking does not have gossipers, either the ones who make it or the ones who take it. There are healthy ways to deal with insecurities, like listening to someone else's nonsense and being amused by it. Walking through the path of self-actualization, you will not have the interest to spend too much time on why gossip comes about and how to deal with it. You learn to ignore it, most of the time. There are only exceptional situations in which you see it as worthy of your time to communicate and make clarifications. Because these types of behaviors and this type of talk gives you the extra baggage we were talking about, you don't want to carry that with you, since it is a source of distraction. Those who come to value you, and those who truly know you will not listen to a person who wants to talk against you.

So, what's the source of your worry? What do you think might happen? Is a little of the people-pleaser still in you? Is a little bit of that "want to be ideal in everyone's eyes" still in you? Some people may judge you because you're a very unique individual in a very positive way. What will happen if they judge you?

But the majority respects you. Looking at your diaries, you have been able to get a great position and respect in society, and that's something to be proud of. As long as you trust yourself and know what you want to do, and are determined to go through the path you have chosen, it will not matter what everyone else thinks. By caring about what others will say, or how they will react, you're giving them power to have a negative effect on your life. There will always be people who are similar to your way of thinking and your style of life, and there are always people who judge others, no matter what.

This reminds me of an interesting and informative story. Every self-actualized person has experienced this feeling of being judged, because they all went beyond and above what others could do. They all knew that the rewards were much more than the downfalls.

There was once a wise man named Nasredeen who lived a simple life. This is one of his stories, with the intention of pointing to what I said before. Nasredeen was riding on his donkey. People started to point at him, judging him for being cruel to animals and making the donkey work too hard. He came down from the donkey and put the donkey on his back. Another group of people started to make fun of him, accusing him of being crazy. Then he decided to get the donkey off his back and walk with him. Yet, another group of people started to make fun of him, questioning his intelligence and asking why he was walking with a donkey, while donkey's job is to give a ride to his owner. Nasredeen, who'd had enough of that, sat on the donkey, went home, and ignored the gossiping. Does it make sense?

Sara: Yes, it makes perfect sense.

Therapist: It's part of the process, Once you go through it, this skill will come with it. Remember, practice makes perfect. You can't give up just because at the beginning it seems to be hard to do. And remember, only a small number of people are able to get to a true sense of self-actualization, not because they don't have the ability, but because they're so drawn into their daily lives, fulfilling basic/animalistic needs, and matters related to it, that they lose focus of what is their real reason for being. And remember, according to Jung, the main reason for being here is to realize the self. This is a continuous process. Now, let me check in with you and see how you feel about what I just said. Then we'll go to your past week.

Sara: My week was very fulfilling. I did a lot of thinking and challenging my irrational beliefs, according to the articles you gave me and what I learned before. I decided to make some changes in these beliefs, and those that were not productive anymore and were just a mimicking factor, but this time taking it more seriously. The more I learn, the more I become aware of myself and become stronger in standing up for what I believe. Knowledge is power, and a true source of inner and outer knowledge makes the process of change easier. Knowing about something automatically takes some of the burden off. The more I become aware, the more I feel secure and happy to be me, because I accept myself, and the less I feel like I have to live by other people's standards. And the more I get that, the more I'm able to feel free from the insecure attachments I had in the name of love.

I challenged myself a lot. I paid attention to of my ways of thinking after something happened, and then asked myself a lot of questions. How is this thought making me feel? Does it make me feel better or worse? What is it doing for me? Is it productive, helping me find a solution, or is it unproductive, just keeping me down all the time? Am I minimizing the positive in my life? Am I overreacting to some aspects of my life? Can I see this in another way? Haven't I experienced something similar before, survived, and moved on? Can I do something about this? If yes, what, and if no, can I learn to accept it?

Asking these questions made me become more aware of what's going on, stopping myself, and changing the pattern. I also noticed that sometimes I acted impulsively, and am learning to be more rational. So, in a way, I acted less impulsively and more reasonably by stopping the harmful thoughts. This was not easy, and I'm still not in full control, but it's getting much easier.

For example, one thing I have truly learned is that you cannot go back and forth with a decision. Some decisions are like a one way street. You have to keep moving forward. With some decisions and the processes they involve, going back and forth is going to waste a lot of valuable energy. With my ex-husband, at times the divorce process got to be extremely difficult. Every time he did something, instead of me sitting down feeling sorry for myself, I reacted, I fought back with my full power and decided that I was going to fight until he got out of my life and stopped disturbing me or my children. During the divorce process, there were times when I really felt overwhelmed, making sure that my boys were not affected by this divorce, and making sure I was still making progress with my profession and charity work while dealing with this very disturbed individual.

At times, the only thing that kept me moving was my spiritual belief; my true sense of inner connection with the creation. I don't know how to explain it, but it was quite an experience, very painful, but rewarding at the same time. It became rewarding because I chose to see it like that. I chose to look at it as a learning experience, rather than an unbearable one.

After all, we are creators, in a sense. We create our own feelings and the way we respond to situations. I *chose* to be a creator who creates constructive situations. I'm not always successful, but I'm trying. I'm not going to deny it; I had some tough times, which were extremely painful. However, I went through them successful and am proud of myself. My children are extremely healthy, both mentally and physically, and everyone who sees them congratulates me for doing such a good job with them. I've devoted my life to make sure I provide the best I can for them.

I guess I created positive thoughts toward a very harsh part of my life. For me, it was the beginning of a new life; one in which I would feel at peace. Fighting all my traditional beliefs related to marriage, changing them, and reacting to them, was a resurfacing experience.

Therapist: Remember, our thoughts could be our number one enemy. They could drag us down, frustrate us, stress us, mentally sicken us, and emotionally make us get stuck at one place in life. If we don't learn to control them, they will be in control, and will be all over the place, running over us. Thoughts are like horses. If you train a horse, she will do the job, give you a ride, and then go to her place to rest until she's ready to be at your service the next day. If the horse is not properly trained, she will run all over you, causing damage and destruction to you and your property. So, we need to learn to train our thoughts. We need to challenge, filter, and control the way we think, because it gives rise to our emotions and our actions. Now, give me a couple of examples of your irrational pattern of thinking.

Sara: For example, "I need to be perfect and good at everything," "I need to please my dad and my family and look like an ideal girl," "I must please everybody," "I should be great at everything I do," "I should not have any weaknesses, because then others might judge me or think something is wrong with me," "I should be better than others," "I should be in control at all times," "I should be close to all my family members, even if I don't like their behavior," " I should not do this because it will make me feel guilty," etc.

Therapist: You're so hard on yourself. All these "shoulds" can take one away from her reality and drown her being.

You had drawn a rigid wall around yourself that would make it very hard for you to live your true life. This person feels such constant pressure that it can get overwhelming. We can replace these "shoulds" with more productive words; words that have less pressure and more function.

Another pattern I see is the use of words like "ideal" and "perfect." You seem to have formed a pattern related to this, and I want to try to get to the root of it. You mentioned some of your childhood experiences, feeling scared at times, and wanting to please your dad a lot. You also mentioned that there were higher expectations for girls than boys in your family. I need to open this up a little more to see where these thoughts are placed in your unconscious, and how they are controlling your way of thinking and behaving today.

Jung described the self's segments as the ego, the personal unconscious, and the collective unconscious. Ego is identified as the conscious mind, which is closely associated with the personal unconscious (anything that is not conscious currently, but could be). Both memories that are remembered and those that have been suppressed are part of this. Jung's third concept, which makes his theory stand out from all others, is called the collective unconscious, which he defines as something of a "psychic inheritance." It's something like knowledge we're all born with, but are unable to be directly conscious of. However, it influences our experiences, thoughts, and behaviors, through our emotions. The more we become aware of these different parts, the more we will be able to become aware of our self, in control of our life, the decisions we make, and how they affect us. Do you have any questions so far? Does this make sense?

Sara: Yes. In my case, I need to become aware of my

ego, which would be something of my child side, the one that acts based on emotions, needs, and impulses. In the article I was reading, it discussed the fact that self-actualized people have a more resourceful perception of reality and accept it more comfortably. This includes recognition of the dishonest person, and the accurate perception of what exists, rather than a distortion of perception by one's needs, based on the child side, so that the adult or the guidance sides are more in control of the person. That is why self-actualized people seem to have more control over their environment and other people. They're not afraid of the unknown, and can tolerate the doubt, uncertainty, and tentativeness accompanying the perception of the new and unfamiliar. What this tells me is that I need to become aware of my conscious side, which is something like the adult side of me, providing guidance, with reason. And then there's a collective conscious side of me that's more like an angelic guidance, with all the wisdom, if I'm able to learn to tune in to it. Right?

Therapist: Yes. Let's go with an example, and do a behavior rehearsal during this session. Let us say you need to make a decision regarding something. What do you want to use as an example?

Sara: Can we use my divorce as an example, because this marriage was one of the biggest mistakes of my life, and it wasn't one that I had much control over, so that's why I want to use it as an example.

Therapist: Sure, let's go with that. You need to make a

decision regarding your divorce. What would your child side, coming from the egoistic part of you, tell you?

Sara: Umm, that I should not get a divorce, because others might judge me or think I'm not perfect. That my father may not approve of it, that I might not be able to handle it, that I must make sacrifices and stay in this marriage, despite constant unhappiness, to make sure others see my life as "ideal," and that I please others.

Therapist: That's good. Your child side works based on emotions and instant gratification. It needs something quickly, without thinking through with reason, and thinking about the short- and long-term consequences. It wants to be like others. It works based on irrational ways of thinking rather than reasonable ones. When we do something based on reason and wisdom, we're automatically more aware of the long-term consequences, we're more determined to do it, and are less worried about what others might think and how others might judge us, because reason and knowledge give power and determination. When we do something based on emotions, since emotions are unstable and are constantly changing, we end up changing our mind, turning into an impulsive human who can't make a decision for herself and has to rely on others to tell her how to live her life and what to do.

It's the same with using irrational thoughts to make our decisions, since there're illogical, they're baseless, and will likely change quickly because they're unstable. The other example would be a side of you before, who, as a woman in her 30's, was still seeking your dad's approval for something as personal as your married life. This is a stage that children need to grow out of. As children, we rely on our parents' guidance with the hope they will lead us toward a healthy growth. As an adult, we can make that choice for ourselves. If we use our adult and guidance side, there's nobody who can make a decision for us better than ourselves. But we have to get there first, and before we get there we could use the guidance of those who have knowledge about the area we have difficulties with. In your case, since you believed your dad had an unhealthy marriage and a lot of irrational ways of traditional thinking about women, you could not use him for guidance regarding your marriage. Another example you used was the concept of what can be categorized as an irrational thinking, specifically related to the word "sacrifice."

An example was what I saw in your diary, "A woman makes sacrifices in her marriage, even if she feels unhappy." We have to know what this word truly means to be able to use it as an excuse. Do we mean compromise or sacrifice? Compromise is a necessary part of any relationship, but sacrifice is an extreme form of compromise.

Remember, extreme forms of anything are not healthy.

We might need to ask ourselves, "Sacrifice for what? Sacrifice for whom, and why? These are the kinds of questions we need to start asking ourselves. What worked decades ago might not work now. Those patterns of thinking were brought up for a reason, and were probably functional for a specific group of people at a specific time, but do they work today, with *our* life? If not, then why are we repeating them and holding on to them?

Thoughts and behaviors should go through the process of progression like everything else in the universe. We cannot be stuck at one place. We have to move on and make changes for continuous growth. In the process, we may have to make some sacrifices for something we believe is a good cause, and is helpful and an element of growth.

Why are we scared of moving out of that destructive comfort zone? Why is change so scary? Why do most people just mimic others?

Okay, I'm going to stop here and check on you. How do you feel?

Sara: I can tell you that my view of life is changing or, I should say, improving, every day. My God, there's so much I don't know. The more I learn, the more I know how blind I was in some areas of my decision-making and life, and how much damage I caused myself because of this blindness. I'm so happy that I'm in a state of waking up, but feel sad to see so many people still sleep or blind to reality and in denial about it. They just move through life without realizing there is something deeper that they need to take pay attention to. There are so many people that may never get out of that state of denial of reality because they are not even aware of their state of being. It seems like we live in a world where everything is labeled so superficially, we get attracted to things impulsively without consideration for short and long term effects on us and others, we judge people based on their first impression or their instant behavior and fail to see the real person inside and the real intention behind the behavior. We define words in a wrong way. For example, in my extended family, the word "sacrifice" meant something totally different than its actual meaning. My understanding of this word, now, is that when something is productive for you, or what you value, when something has a positive effect on your state of being, you make compromises.

This is the same in a marriage. When you marry someone who you think is contributing to your physical, mental, and spiritual health, you surrender in some areas that you feel helps your relationship, to help your partner feel good about the relationship. The way I was brought up, sacrifice meant that no matter what the other person does to you in a marriage, you suck it up and don't let anyone know about it. This referred only to women, of course. You do whatever you can to stay in the marriage, even if you feel like it is mentally and emotionally hurting you. That was defined as "sacrifice," and it may have been imposed upon people to believe that it is a positive thing.

Now, using my reason and going up the ladder of self-growth, I can see things more clearly, I can see that it was not sacrifice, but being weak and playing the victim's role. I saw so many women with potential who just did not grow, I saw so many suffering, but without knowing what was going on with them. I decided that I wasn't going to sacrifice for something that is damaging to me. In a way, I should say, I was damaging myself.

Therapist: What do you mean by damaging yourself?

Sara: How I blocked myself from what I could be and feel, and how I prevented myself from growing to my full potential, because of some of my ways of thinking and behaviors. How I wasted so many opportunities for growth to please others. How I lived with severe anxiety, and thought that was normal.

Since my divorce, and my last separation, in which my ex-husband moved out of the house and I didn't have to deal with him physically, I feel like I have a free soul. I feel like I have blossomed. I feel like I can do anything. I finished my thesis, I wrote a book, I finished my drawing, I'm on my way to achieving many of my goals that I was never motivated to achieve, before. I feel more like myself. I feel less anxious and more alive.

Even though my ex-husband still tries to hurt me any way he can, I feel like I don't pay attention to that anymore, or at least I'm learning to not to pay attention. I've totally shifted my focus away from him, and focus more on the solution than on the problem. You know Doctor, I feel like I've always lived the life of tenderness with him, but me and him were just a bad combination. Now, to think of it, I've made some mistakes, but who doesn't? I never made a mistake intentionally. It was always for a reason or from lack of knowledge. My mistakes seem much smaller than those I see around me. These days, I think more of my childhood memories. I never thought about it, or only thought about a couple of good ones. Now, I've learned that it was because I had suppressed these memories. The more I think of them, the more I'm able to accept them, and feel like I can move on with them now. I feel like I'm processing them, and as a result my baggage is getting lighter. I feel like they're not hurting me, but are a part of me. I remember vividly the day my ex-husband's family came to ask for me, how I was not asked how I felt, how I did not even see him, how we were told many lies, that he was highly educated, had a good job, had a house, and had never been with another woman. That was important for me, back then. My parents didn't do much to help with guiding me and supporting me with making the right decision. I was, in a way, pushed into marrying someone I hardly knew. Shortly after, I knew I'd made a mistake. There was something about the way he was acting that I just knew he was not the right man for me, but there was no way out for me. I was very young, almost a teenager, immature emotionally, but intelligent, living with anxiety, and feeling lonely. I knew there was no way for a divorce, so I decided to do my best to make it work. I ignored and kept to myself all the lies; the fact that he wasn't making any money, that we didn't have enough to go through the month-to-month cost of living, the fact that his education wasn't what they said, that he had been with a number of woman before me, and that he'd been married before, the fact that he completely ignored me emotionally and was very flirtatious toward other woman, the fact that at times he was abusive, controlling, and obsessed, but worst of all was constantly changing his mind about what he wanted, not with reason, but to prove something. I felt like I was living with a little boy who had no emotional boundaries. I remember when I asked him, crying, why he hid his previous marriage away from me.

His response was, "Oh come on, don't make a big deal out of every little thing I told you." And then he started to laugh. That's the way he was. He laughed and cried at the wrong times and the wrong places. Oh, how I have so many examples, some of which I still don't feel comfortable sharing, not even with you.

Therapist: Try to tell me more about some of those memories. You're doing a marvelous job of letting them out, and letting out these unspoken words.

Sara: I followed your instructions and brought some of my childhood pictures. I started to look at them carefully, and remembered my childhood as it really was, not as I wanted it to be. I'm trying to learn to make this a part of my life. In order to learn about myself, I have to learn about my past and where I came from. Only then can I understand myself better and make any changes I wish to. Avicenna says, and I quote, "God is knowledge; he is knowing; and he is being known." Since God has knowledge of his own essence, and since God is one, it follows that the essence of God is knowledge. Knowledge means that he knows himself, and is known by himself.

So, I'm getting more comfortable with the process. I see it as continuous. It's not something one does once, and it's over. It's just the beginning. A change I've noticed is that I've started being more honest with myself. Somehow, it seems like this honesty with myself was missing because I was encouraged to hide my true feelings. It seemed to me that denial and avoidance were rewarded during my childhood, not intentionally, but because they didn't know about the process. I remember craving for my mother's love and attention, and her coldness and restrictive behavior. I remember her openly favoring my brothers over me. I remember her constantly talking about my dad to me, and expecting me to agree with her. If I took his side, it would make my mother so mad at me. I do remember that she, deep down inside, loved me, and cared, to a point, about my school and my education. But I specifically remember a lot of lonely moments. I also remember getting close to my aunts and my cousins, to get love from them. I was my aunts' and uncles' favorite, and was popular for being super kind and lovable. But now I see our relationship as more superficial. I knew how to gain love and give it. Up to a point, some of my childhood love was received from these family members, but it was because I was constantly giving them love and not expecting anything in return. Despite all of this, I remember feeling like I was the luckiest kid in my extended family, because they all had their own set of problems. So, in a way I didn't dare complain, because how can you complain when you have more than others? How can you acknowledge the hard parts of your life, when others have it so much worse around you? This was the way I used to think. Now, I try to see it as it is. I try to see the negative parts as well as the positive, acknowledging them instead of denying and suppressing them, and accepting them and moving on. If in this process I feel mad at somebody, and they're not ready to hear my point of view and have the same pattern of behavior as the ones that damaged me in my earlier years, I don't push myself into getting close to them. I will go with my own pace, with my own heart, to see when I'm ready to get close to them. And I know that it may never be, but this way I feel less resentment and less anger and hate toward those who hurt me. I just want to protect myself to make sure I won't be hurt any more. Do you hear me Doctor?

Therapist: I hear you. As children, we humans use a number of defense mechanisms to protect ourselves, mentally and physically. As we mature, however, we need to balance these mechanisms. Two of these mechanisms are projection and denial.

Projection is an unconscious psychological mechanism. We project parts of ourselves that we deny the existence of onto others. There are many hidden parts to us, some of which are immature because we haven't paid attention to them. The reason for these hidden parts could be that we're constantly trying to look a certain way and keep our image together, causing denial of our different parts. Our intention is to be accepted by others, family, society, etc. We should know that the fact that these parts are hidden within unconscious does not make them inactive. On the other hand, it gives them more power over us. They affect all our behaviors and thinking patterns. Once we become aware of these parts of ourselves, and start processing and balancing them, we will be able to control them, rather than them having control over us.

Carl Jung said, "Everyone carries a shadow, and the less it is embodied in the individual's conscious life, the blacker and denser it is. At all counts, it forms an unconscious snag, thwarting our most well-meant intentions."

To refer this to self-actualization, remember that acceptance of self, others, and nature is a characteristic of these individuals, and doesn't happen in an instant. They have to go through the process of self-purification. Self-actualizing persons are not ashamed or guilty about their human nature, with its deficiencies, limitations, weaknesses, and drawbacks. Nor are they critical of these features in others. They respect and value themselves, and that's why they are able to respect and value others in its true form. They are honest, open, and genuine, without fakeness or facade. They are concerned about discrepancies between what is, and what might be or should be, in themselves, others, and society. Another characteristic of a self-actualized person is the quality of detachment and the need for privacy, which leads them to enjoy solitude and privacy. A self-actualized person does not get as disturbed as others by upsetting events. To some, she may appear to be asocial, but that's not the case at all. This is due to her sense of security and self sufficiency, not her inability to socialize.

Also, self-actualized people have a strong sense of autonomy, which gives them a sense of independence of culture and environment. While they are dependent on others for the satisfaction of the basic needs of love, safety, respect, and belongingness, they are not dependent for their main satisfactions of the world, or other people, or culture, or what is called an extrinsic satisfaction. Rather they are dependent on their own development and continued growth, based on their own capabilities and assets. Carl Rogers refers to this as the internal locus of control.

Sara: This is very meaningful. In a world where many people seem to be something that is not their real self, this makes so much sense. That's why some psychologists say only about 2% get to be self-actualized. I truly do not know of anyone, personally, who is there yet. So much damage in today's world, so many selfish acts in the name of kindness, so much crossing other people's boundaries, racism, discrimination, misuse of power; all that come from people to people, and this pretty much explains it. I guess this is what the prophets were trying to communicate to us, but with their time's language and their people's level of understanding. Of course it would have been hard, during their time, to discuss the term self-actualization, but they opened the way for such a term and such a process.

It's amazing how just becoming aware of something makes a whole world of difference. I see many so-called religious people who are the most ignorant of all, using their religious beliefs to judge others and label them as good or evil. I see others who think they're on top of the world because they have education or money, but they're full of personality disorders and aren't even aware of it. I see so many angry people who put their anger on others and damage their surroundings. I was coaching a lady a while ago, and we were working on self-value. She was a beautiful woman who wanted to take porno pictures and sell them. She asked me what I thought about that decision. I didn't just give her my opinion. I showed her why I had that opinion, and what effects this behavior might have on her surroundings. I feel like people are tired of being preached at. We have a lot of preachers who don't know what they are talking about, and don't practice what they preach.

I think we should encourage and teach people to experience what they want to learn. For example, with this lady I showed her three separate stories of the Detective Series in which a perpetrator had raped and killed other women, and they all had some form of porno movie, magazine, alcohol, and/or drugs found in their house. So, I asked her to look at how these types of pictures affect a person who is already predisposed to it, and this person then goes about destroying lives, families, and damaging the society.

Reading through the details of the stories and how her decision for posing for these magazines might have a negative affect, and how she could find healthier ways to find jobs and make money without having to misuse and devalue her most valuable possession, which is her body, made her change her mind totally. She learned to value her body as a beautiful creation, full of amazing designs, rather than a piece of meat for a perpetrator's joy.

There are some things you can't buy with any amount of money, and one of them is your self-worth and self-value. So, in a way, she experienced how her behavior might affect others. After seeing and becoming knowledgeable about it, there was no need for further explanation; she simply did not want to do it.

Therapist: That was a good example of how becoming aware of the deeper layers of a behavior can help the person in the decision-making process. Sometimes humans become so occupied with gratifying instant impulses and gaining short-term results that they don't bother looking at the long term effects of their decisions on themselves and on others. Looking at the pyramid of self-actualization, many people are trapped in the first, second, and third layers; see, take a look at this chart (for the reader please look at the self-actualization pyramid provided in the first chapter).

So, referring back to our previous discussion, tell me what you see as different parts of you? What have you discovered, looking at your childhood pictures and keeping a diary?

Sara: That I'm not perfect and don't want to be, because there is no such a thing as perfect. The world is continuously changing. Therefore, it can't get to a place labeled as perfect. I think the world should be in balance, not perfect; I think trying to reach balance at any given time is the true perfection. I want to see it as wholeness, finding my whole self, and aiming toward actualizing myself.

The fact that I tried to please others made me want them to categorize me as a perfect person. I focused too much on the outside world, and lost my inner self in the process. Deep down inside, other people' compliments felt good, because I had my own insecurities and wanted to hear others say positive things about me. So, I tried to act in a way to keep that image at the cost of my own true peace.

I pretended to be perfect and to have a perfect life, if there even is such a thing. In a world that's changing constantly, how can one be perfect or complete? It just doesn't work like that. Looking back and around with more awareness, I realize that I don't know of anyone who is perfect, or who has it all. I realize that the mask I had on was just a mask, that I was dishonest with myself, that I was a people-pleaser. That I did not value myself in a true sense, I just pretended that I did. Deep down inside, I was insecure and attracted people into my life who fed this insecurity, and then I felt misused by them.

No one can truly abuse you if you do not let them to do so.

We are not victims if we do not choose to be.

Many things are within our power, especially in parts of the world where freedom is much more encouraged and woman's rights are more acknowledged. We should do our best not to let others take advantage of us. I have found it doable for a woman to keep her womanly characteristics, like being kind, being a caregiver, and being the nurturer, but at the same time being powerful, not in a way of aggressiveness but in a way of assertiveness. This is something I'm working on, to be more assertive and to find a balance between my emotional side vs. my rational one. So, referring back to your question, looking through my childhood memories, I can see that I had good moments, but also some bad ones. But, as I said, these days I think more of the bad ones and don't know why.

Therapist: Well, that could be a normal response to your acknowledging these suppressed memories. You mentioned that you've already thought about the good times, so you may not feel the need, for now, to think about them, though it's always good to keep a balance and see it clearly.

But, all those suppressed memories have been buried inside you for so long, and now they're rushing to come out. This may make you feel overwhelmed. That's why it's important to share them with me and do the processing while you're with me. It's also very important to take constant breaks from this process and find ways to relax.

At this time, I encouraged Sara to relax her body and imagine her childhood.

Sara: I remember my brother hitting me, sometimes, over small things. I remember feeling like I didn't have anyone to defend me. My mom usually gave me a signal that I deserved it, one way or the other, maybe because I talked back or tried to defend myself. The strange thing was that there were a lot of times when I saw my brother being protective of me, too.

The only person in my family who hugged and kissed me was my dad. This was very much dependent on his mood, but when he was in a good one he would kiss me and show me love and kind words. That felt great, and maybe that's why I took his side over my mom's. And maybe that's why I ended up trying as hard as I could to please him. One side of me felt very sorry for him. He had much potential, but his family imposed unreasonable expectations on him. He always believed them and gave in. He didn't get much love from my mom, and didn't feel like he came home to a kind, loving, and nurturing wife. I guess he was in complete denial about many things. My parents' fights were traumatizing to me.

Therapist: Before we go on any longer, I have to remind you that our time is about to be over. I need you to relax and take a couple of deep breaths, leave your thoughts here in this office, and only pay attention to them when you need to. I don't want you to be constantly thinking about this, and need you to focus on the process, not the problems. Once you focus on the process, the whole healing course becomes more productive.

At this point I took Sara through a visual imaginary process and we ended the session with a series of homework for her to go through.

Session 5

The following session, we began with casual conversation.

Therapist: How are you feeling?

Sara: I don't know, Doctor. I feel a combination of feelings and just...

Sara could not identify her feelings. She asked if she could read something she'd written during the past week. I encouraged her to do so.

Sara: You know Doctor, this comes from my heart, in its true sense. From my deepest level of being. Here we go. There have been times when I felt like I was at the end of my rope, nothing else to see, nowhere else to go, it seemed dark, it seemed empty, it seemed like it was all a huge void. I sat down, I bended my knee, I was staring at something, but didn't know what it was, I had a feeling, but couldn't really feel my own feeling, I don't know how to explain it. It's hard to explain in words, since it's not a physical experience. I felt like crying, but didn't have any tears. It seemed like even my tears were tired and had given up.

I sat down, lonely, empty, cold handed, tired and . . . all of a sudden, here it came again, don't ask me what, I can't explain with words, it was something harmonious, enjoyable, peaceful, and just perfect. It seeded a hope in me, again. It was as if this blissfulness was talking to me. It seemed like it was a part of me talking to my self; to a deeper part of me that I had ignored most of my life. But it was always with me, just wanting me to pay attention. This harmonious being was not really a separate being; it was an unseen part of my consciousness. It was protecting me, it had all the answers, and it was connected to me as nothing else.

I'd been looking for it outside, but it was here all along. What a feeling, first confusion, then overwhelmed, then non-stop cry for the love I felt, then begging for forgiveness for my ignorance of not paying attention, then a sense of calmness, then hope. A hopeful feeling that gave me the power to believe that as long as I do the right thing, with knowledge, with reason, and with the help of my heart's message, then I will be more than just okay. Then I will walk toward getting to know myself and getting to reach my full potential; the ability that I came to this world with, but was unaware of, the ability that makes it easier for me to walk through my path. I don't need to imitate anyone else, I don't need to be someone else, I don't need to live according to someone else's patterns of thinking, I have all the answers right here. I only need to pay attention to it. I only need to become aware of it, in its true sense. It's time to practice, no more preaching, start the work. As I started to take each step, I could feel the changes in me, I could feel the seeds that started to blossom in me. I would not change this feeling for anything in the world. I don't even think it's a feeling, but I'll call it that because I don't know what else to call it.

Therapist: This is touching. It seems like, sometimes, you can better identify your feelings when you're writing. I really enjoyed it and encourage you to share your writings with me whenever you like. Now, you said you had a combination of feelings. How long have you had this? Was it just today, or during the whole week?

Sara: I don't know how to explain it. I don't want anyone to think that I'm turning into some form of antisocial person. However, it's hard for me to really connect with many people I used to connect with, and it's getting harder. I mean, it's easy to find friends. I'm likable, and people want to be my friends. However, it seems like I just cannot find many people whose company I truly enjoy, people I can have a good time with. It seems like many people's definition of a good time is very superficial, and I just can't accept and can't enjoy that. Many times, I go to spend time with someone, and I don't feel like I enjoyed it. They either gossip about someone else, talk about very superficial and pointless things, or want to spend time doing what seems meaningless to me, and I end up feeling my time was wasted. I don't know, at the same time, I do feel lonely, sometimes. I love people; I crave people, and want to be with them. However, I end up seeing some of them acting in ways that are damaging to themselves and to the world, not in a judging way, but I feel bad and don't enjoy my time. I care much more about quality than quantity. I've become very selective when getting close to people. I want to have productive relationships rather than just killing time. I don't want to spend time with people who seem ignorant. I want to enjoy my time, have fun, learn, and feel good about the time spent.

Therapist: I can see that you're feeling confused by these emotions. I can see your hand shaking when you're talking about this. Your voice starts to change, too. All these are signs of potential anxiety. It seems to me that as your level of awareness increases, you become more conscious of your surroundings, but at the same time you have to learn new ways to deal with the deficiencies you see around you.

Because there is no such a thing as perfect, everything is constantly changing, so there's no way to identify something as perfect. You said the same thing. The world is composed of opposites, which we humans identify as bad or good. Bad or good are categorizations, not explanations; they're relative to the situation. The same is true with other people and other parts of our surroundings. There are things we see that we feel comfortable with, and ones we don't feel as comfortable toward. We have to find ways to be able to deal, in healthy ways, with those who we don't feel comfortable about. We can't get a sense of frustration every time we see something we don't approve of. It will damage us. Only then is one able to observe rather than judge. When one looks with a judgmental view, because one does not think about all the facts that led to that behavior, one feels frustrated because s/he starts judging the person rather than observing the behavior. Now, I understand that there are some behaviors that are extremely repulsive to us. All I'm saying is that we can't change the person who is behaving that way, but we can change ways we deal with it so we won't get damaged by it. What do you think about this?

Sara: It does make sense to me, but it's hard to do. So, let's say for example, what if someone in your family does something that you don't approve of? What's the most reasonable way to deal with that?

Therapist: First of all, I like the fact that you're using the word "reasonable" more and more often. Once a person decides to work on herself, this word has to become a part of her daily dialogue with herself. Becoming a reasonable person means working through problems based on facts and reason, and also based on what effects it will have on us in the long term, according to our priorities. It isn't just based on impulses and feelings.

In other words, our guidance and adult sides should overcome our child side for making decisions. Feelings are temporary matters that change from one state to another. Usually, when we act on feelings, after the feeling changes, we regret the act. An example would be when we get angry and act impulsively, hurting ourselves or someone else in the process. Now, this same anger can be used as a signal to look into why we're feeling this, and what's giving us this feeling. If our reason tells us that it's someone trying to hurt us, and that's why our emotion is giving us this sense of anger, then, after calming down, we use our thinking process, based on our reasoning, to come up with the best possible long-term solution to respond to this feeling.

Now, if we can't come up with a solution by ourselves, there's always professional help, but we don't just get help from anybody; we get it from those who have actual knowledge about it. The same is true with anything else. If you have questions about your physical health you ask a medical doctor. This is a very sensitive area that we have to be careful with. Now, let's go back to your question, give me a specific example related to your situation.

Sara: Okay, let me give you this example, since it's constantly in my mind and I don't know how to deal with it. My relationship with my father, during my divorce. I haven't been talking to him, just because of the way he reacted. I thought his reaction was very selfish, and was deeply hurt by it.

At this point Sara started to cry. I let her feel her emotion and let it out. Crying, sometimes, is the best form of therapy. Just feeling the emotion, acknowledging it, and trying to deal with it after it comes, rather than denying it. Learning this process is one of the most important parts of therapy, healing, or self discovery. Sara took a deep breath and continued:

Sara: You know Doctor, I've always idealized my dad. I think I told you a little bit about that. I was in such denial that he, like everyone else, had weaknesses. I got so deeply drawn into the habit of defending him every time my mom was talking against him that I lost the truth in the process. It was like a habit. I defended him and idealized him, and didn't take time to think of the truth, until my divorce came. That was the first time I decided to stand up for myself and go with what I thought was the right thing for me to do. This was against what my dad wanted, and that was when I saw his other side, the side you explained as the shadow. That side was so damaging to me. I felt like I was in a state of shock and disbelief when I woke up and got out of the denial phase.

I thought, Oh my God, what a fool I was to think that he loved me.

You know. I mean, I know he still loves me, but his definition of love is very different from mine, and that's where we separate. His definition of love is more of what was explained by a psychologist as the "anxious attachment."

My definition is having a "connection," in a healthy sense, or at least I'm trying to learn that. I can't say I'm totally there, I can see that I still have some work to do, but learning about it just made so much sense, and it was like an awakening. Knowledge is power. I did want to ask you about it because, somehow, hearing it from you, personally, makes it all more practical.

Therapist: As I can see from your experiences, the sense of healthy connection comes as the person learns to face her insecurities, trusts herself more, and gets to know herself. We attach to others, as children, to caregivers, and to adults, because we feel helpless, and because we need help to survive, we also attach to others to have our needs fulfilled. We will do whatever we can to hold on to these attachments. But, as we grow, if the process is done in a normal, healthy and nurturing environment, then we will learn to grow more and more independent, more as our own individual self, but still connected to that sense of belonging, if we feel that it's beneficial for us.

Let me use an example. As a little girl, you wanted your dad's love and attention because you weren't getting that, (or so you thought), from your mom. So, you were trying to fulfill that need through your dad. To gain that, you tried to please him to get his attention and love. You got some of it. As you grew older, you were supposed to learn ways to become more and more dependent on yourself to build on your self-esteem, and to fill out your insecurities. You were not able to do that as well as you wanted to, because you were still attached to your dad; still trying to please him even though you were not a child anymore. Therefore, in the process of trying to please him, you forgot your real self's needs and cravings. At the same time, your needs had changed, and the childhood love and attention he was giving you was not enough.

Sara: Yes, that makes sense. What do you make of my father? Do you think he loves me?

Therapist: I don't know who your father is, so I can't tell whether his way of loving is your way of craving love. But, what I know is that once you learn to be your true self, once you learn to accept yourself as you are. Once you work through your insecurities, and find a balance between your child self and your adult self, it will be easier for you to find a reasonable way to satisfy your need of a relationship with your father in a way that makes sense to you and is healthy for you, not what others say you have to do.

You also have to consider the fact that you're stepping out of an old habitual behavior and into your new zone. That means you're leaving your comfort zone. We talked about the comfort zone last time.

But what's important is that your dad was part of that comfort zone, with a set of expectations from his daughter that she was following. Some of these expectations were very unreasonable. Now, for him, all of a sudden, that same daughter is moving away from that comfort zone. He will feel the change. He may get scared, angry, and want to pull you back in, because he isn't used to the new you. But, as you move farther away from that zone, and as time goes on, he may finally come to a point where he may accept the whole thing. Whether he will approve of it or not, we don't know, but he will probably accept it, one way or the other.

He has to accept it, if you are determined. But the point is that once you walk through the self-actualization process, it's only you who knows what's best for you. By then, your child side will not be hurt as much by your dad's disapproval, because your adult side will be approving and fulfilling that child's need. In a way, by self-actualization, you've been able to find a balance between your different selves to fulfill each need within yourself. It's all about self-sufficiency. You will become, in some ways, a self-sufficient piece of work. That's when we say you will still have that sense of connection to others and to the world, but it will be more of a healthy connection rather than a damaging attachment, meaning that you will connect when you feel like you can benefit or can be benefited, but can remove yourself when you feel like it's damaging.

Relationships, in any form or shape, have to be symbiotic, not parasitic, meaning that everyone involved should benefit and feel like they are gaining as much as giving. This is a very personal decision, based on the person's needs and personality, and the level of psychological and coral maturity they're at. Now, related to your dad, where do you think you are, based on what we talked about?

Sara: I don't really know. I feel like he's my dad and I have to have a relationship with him. That's one side of me. There are some good times with him that I remember, and there are times that I've enjoyed being with him. I do know that I never shared my true feelings with him, and always wanted him to think that I had it all. In a way, I didn't want to be a burden on him, so I never shared my painful experiences with him. Even as a child, I tried very hard not to be a weight on my family. I always kept my problems to myself, and didn't want to make them sad, or maybe I had too much pride to tell them I had a problem. Also, I didn't feel like they would help me.

Therapist: What do you mean by a weight?

Sara: Well, I mean making them worry about me.

Therapist: I see, go on.

Sara: Right now, I have some sadness about the fact that my dad was not there for me, the way I needed him to be. However, I don't have any angry feeling toward him. I do have this intense feeling of sadness that he uses prescribed opiate and abuses its use and at this point there does not seem to be a way out of it for him, and it has affected his judgment and his personality. I don't know. Should I have anger toward him? Should I forgive him? What do you think?

Therapist: I think I need to know more before I can help you answer this question within yourself. Therefore, we'll wait on that. But what I can tell you is that you also have a part in this. You mentioned that you've always tried to show them you "have it all," and did not want to be an emotional burden on them. So, they were not aware of your situation.

Now, all this is new to them, and to your dad, and for him to understand your decision and your situation takes some time. I'm assuming that he will understand it, and may even ask you for forgiveness, which may not be direct, because of his beliefs, but indirect, so you have to get prepared for that and know what your response will be.

Nevertheless, what I can tell is that your dad probably reacted to your situation according to his level of understanding and maturity. He gave what he had been given. In other words, he gave you, as a father, what he'd been given by his environment. He cannot give what he has not learned. You cannot expect a first grader to comprehend the fifth grader's material, not because he is not capable, but because he has not reached that level yet.

However, that doesn't mean that you should let your father make decisions for you. That's were boundaries come into play. You communicate them to your father the best way you can, and expect him not to cross your boundaries anymore. Hopefully, as time goes on he will learn to respect that, even if he doesn't understand it.

If he doesn't disrespect your boundaries, you act accordingly, making sure that no one, not even your father, would intentionally or unintentionally keep on hurting you. Related to your feelings, you said you don't have any angry feelings anymore, but sadness. This process, for you, is the same as a grieving process. You see, our mental processing is an amazing creation that works so well and is so well-designed. If we learn about it, we'll be able to deal with life much better, and enjoy life, with all it throws at us.

The grieving process means the process our psych goes through when we feel like we've lost something. This could be a loved one, something valuable to us, something we had hoped for and worked for but didn't get, or we did get it, but then lost it. This could also be something we expected to have but never did. At this point, your grieving process is the love of your father the way you needed it. Does it make sense so far?

Sara: Kind of. So, the love, the way I wanted it or, on the other hand, my definition of love according to my need, was something I expected to have but did not get, and as a result my psych is going to go through a grieving process. Right?

Therapist: Yes. So, your child side feels like she's lost something, perhaps a caring dad or mom she expected to have. We'll focus on the dad for now. So, after becoming aware of it, you go through the stages of grieving, which are denial, anger, sadness, and acceptance. There may be a couple of more feelings that are thrown at you in between these, but they're the general ones. So, at the beginning, you deny that there's anything wrong. You just think things like "everything is okay," "this is how he should act, and his reaction is normal," "this is what everyone experiences."

Then, after you pass the denial phase and become aware of the reality of the situation and see the fact that your dad should have been there for you, and that his reaction damaged you, comes the anger phase. You're angry at your dad, perhaps at the world, and you're asking why he has to act like that, why isn't he there for me when I need him, why does he only think of himself and his reputation when he should be thinking of my happiness, too.

After this anger phase comes a sadness which is what you're experiencing right now. As time passes, you process this as well, and then comes the acceptance phase. You'll be able to accept the situation as it is, that is if you have been successful in not letting him cross your boundaries again. You will feel a sense of calm, and will move on with your life with clear boundaries so you won't have to experience that painful feeling again. Does it make sense?

Sara: It makes perfect sense. How long should each phase take?

Therapist: It depends on the person and the situation. Hopefully, not too long. Probably a few months at each phase is more of a normal route. There has to be a balance between the phases. The fewer blockages a person has, the more balanced it will be. There's no specific number, but no one wants to be stuck at one phase for too long, because life is waiting. Okay, now it's time for this question referring back to what you were saying. You said you feel a sense of intense sadness. What is the sadness related to? What did your father, specifically, do that makes you feel this way?

Sara: Well, let me tell you the story of the past few years, and then I'll go back, if you feel that would help. Is that okay?

Therapist: Sure. Whatever feels comfortable to you is what I want to hear.

Sara: During my continuously conflicting marriage, as I

was getting more educated and more aware of the damage it was causing me, and how I was living in disharmony with my inner needs, I got out of denial more. At the same time, my ex-husband, who for the first time had found a good job and a stable salary, was abusing this money power, and was becoming more passively controlling. I want to spend more time on my marriage, later, but now I'll focus on my dad. About four years ago, we separated and were sleeping in separate rooms. I wanted so badly to get a divorce, but it just didn't seem possible. It seemed so scary, and too far out of my reach. I had many obstacles in my way, and the fact that my children were too young, and I didn't know what I was going to do. So, I started to work harder and harder to make the marriage work, but started to have a lot of inner anger and resentment toward my ex-husband. We got back together, I don't even know how, we just did. Then, about three years ago, we separated again.

It seemed like no matter how hard I worked, things would seem okay for a short time and would bounce back to frustration. It seemed like the problem was designed wrong so there was no solution for it. This time, I felt like, this was it. Even if my ex-husband begged on is knees, I was going to stay strong and determined and would stand up to my decision.

But, once again, my weakness and anxiety overcame me, and I let others make decisions for me. I got back with him one more time. Every time, I was taking a part of myself away from me. Every time, I was feeling a little less of value for not being able to stand up for what I really wanted. I don't know what I was thinking. Every time, I was fooled by his lies and manipulation that he was going to make it work. Every chance I gave him, he went back to his true self. It seemed like I could never change him. It was his true identity, and he would re-shape back to his true identity no matter how hard he tried to cover it.

It took me a long time to discover that you can never change someone's true identity. They are who they are, and if they're not really willing to change, there's nothing you can do. My ex-husband is emotionally very immature and unstable, and I could never trust him. He says something and does something else, he constantly lies, and isn't even aware of it, he constantly thinks he is the victim, even when he's being abusive, he always wants more and gives the least, has no reason, and changes in extreme forms.

Doctor, before I go any further, why is that? Why is it that some people like to look like victims? I see myself and how much pride I have. I never let anyone feel sorry for me. I hate it when someone wants to feel sorry for me. I like it when they want to support me, but not looking down at me like. "Oh, poor Sara." But he loves that. He would do anything for others to say, "Oh, poor him, what a good boy." Why is that?

Therapist: Well, there are a number of reasons. Based on your conversation and your diary, the first thing that seems an obvious sign of your ex-husband is that he seems to be impulsive. People who turn over their lives to their own impulses are more likely to trust their first impressions, absolutely.

As one person said during his therapy, "I'm intuitive, and know quickly when someone is lying to me." The word "quickly" could be an impulse problem and could mean "without thinking."

Some people, like your ex-husband, may act on their

hunches immediately. They just don't have patience, or the knowledge that they have to think things through before acting on them. Studies indicate that this inability to self-regulate could be, partially, due to genetic variation, as well as early childhood wounds. These individuals may be very needy, misread other people's motives, and be impulsive in response. And a reason for the second part of your story could be that his child side is strongly active, and that it wasn't nourished properly when he was a child. He's still stuck in that stage, and still wanting to get that nourishment, but in the wrong ways, which cause damage to him and to his surroundings. He just doesn't know that he's being damaging, because he's living through his primitive, or child, side. For example, he might do a lot of work to try to look like the victim so people will feel sorry for him. That's a form of manipulation. Or, another example would be him putting a spy on your computer, which is against any moral or legal law. This is a way for him to covertly control you. That means that he has a lot of inner anger, which he doesn't show directly, but expresses indirectly.

Living with a passive-aggressive (covertly aggressive) manipulator who wants to look like a victim is very hard and challenging. I'm not saying, at this point, that he's all of this, but from some of your explanations, he could have some of these characteristics. Let me explain that there are two basic types of aggression: overt and covert. When one is determined to have something and they are open, direct, and obvious in their manner of fighting for it, their behavior is best labeled *overtly aggressive*. On the other hand, when one is out to "win," dominate, or control, but in a subtle, underhanded, or deceptive enough way to hide their true intentions, their behavior is labeled as covertly aggressive.

Now, someone who avoids overt displays of aggression, but intimidates others into giving them what they want, is a manipulator. A manipulator who tries to look like the victim may have the following characteristics.

One is that this person's aggression is not obvious. Our gut may tell us that they're fighting for something, struggling to overcome us, gain power, or have their way, and we find ourselves unconsciously on the defensive. But because we can't point to clear, objective evidence that they're aggressing against us, we can't readily validate our feelings.

Second, the tactics manipulators use can make it seem like they're hurting, caring, defending; almost anything but fighting. These tactics are hard to recognize as merely clever ploys. They always make just enough sense to make a person doubt their gut hunch that they're being taken advantage of or abused. The tactics not only make it hard for you to consciously and objectively tell that a manipulator is fighting, but they also keep you consciously on the defensive.

These features make them highly effective psychological weapons, to which anyone can be vulnerable. It's hard to think clearly when someone has you emotionally on the run. I recommend the book, *Dealing with Manipulative People, Wolf in Sheep's Clothing,* By George K. Simon, PhD. In this book he provided a good explanation of these people. I am guessing that you may be able to see more cause for your anxiety.

Sara: Oh my God! You explained my ex-husband so well. That's exactly him. Word for word. What a good feeling to know that what you thought of a person has a reasonable explanation. It's so very hard to live with these people. I think it gives you anxiety.

Therapist: Yes, these types of people are the hardest to live with. Because if someone is openly aggressive, you can confront them and come up with a solution, either to work on it or move on, or you may even want to make a clear decision that you don't want to live with them anymore. But with a passive-aggressive manipulator, making a decision and figuring out what's going on, one has to be extremely sharp and open, and familiar with psychological aspects of a person. This is a very hard task. Even though you're a smart and intelligent woman, you still couldn't figure it out for many years of struggling with what's going on, but were feeling tense and anxious.

Sara: Exactly, I was so anxious. Now my children have the same feelings with him. They have some of the same experiences with him that I did. But theirs is much less severe, because we talk about their feelings a lot. Also, they've learned ways to deal with this. Some of the things they know now, it took me twenty years to learn. I guess because we're the ones who lived with him. Oh, my God! I'm speechless! But the difference with my children is that I've taught them ways to deal with it, I've gotten the kind of extra support they need to be able to deal with his behavior.

At this point, Sara seemed to have been overwhelmed by all the information she was processing. When a person's level of awareness increases, there is a series of stimulations that accompany it. The person needs to learn skills to deal with it. As the old saying goes, "Once you know the road is one-way, there's no turning back." Once the truth of a situation reveals itself to you through knowledge and factual information, you become more aware of what's going on and how to respond. I encouraged Sara to take a break and continue with her feelings when she was ready.

Sara: I feel better now. I just have to process all this. I have a sense of excitement, but fear at the same time.

Therapist: What is the fear related to? Where does it come from?

Sara: Fear of the changes I'm about to make. As I become more aware of the deeper layers of the truth, I'm thinking of all the changes I have to make to become more of myself. I see many mistakes that I've made in the name of sacrifice, kindness, people-pleasing, and labeling the behaviors as something positive, even though they were not. If they were positive, they would not be damaging me at the end, right?

I mean, why did I let others control me, one way or the other? Specifically, why did I let my husband control and manipulate me emotionally, and sometimes even physically, and forgave and forgot all in the name of sacrifice? It wasn't a sacrifice. Sacrifice to whom, to what? Don't I owe it to myself, first, in order to be able to have it for others? I mean, I've always heard from scholars, including yourself, that until you truly learn to know your true self and pay attention to who you are, and how to respect your boundaries, there's no way you can be of any true help to others.

Therapist: That's true, and is something we'll learn more about during these therapy sessions. We'll learn why that is, and how the process works. There are reasons for everything. We just have to put time and effort into learning them. To refer back to your question of why you let others control or abuse you, let me explain something, and then ask you a question.

The abuser may use many different types of abuse to assert his or her power, and the overall framework in which the abuse occurs may follow a pattern called the Cycle of Violence. This cycle includes the first phase in which the abuse expresses itself in a variety of ways and patterns. It might be ongoing, non-stop, or stop and start. The first phase of one of these patterns is the tension-building phase, then the actual abuse, and then a calm phase in which the abuser/controller tries to make up. This make-up phase is called the honeymoon phase. Does it make sense?

Sara: So, the first phase is the abuse phase?

Therapist: The first phase is the tension-building phase, which includes increasing anger on the part of the abuser, coupled with attempts by the abused to avoid abuse. On the other hand, the abused may attempt to bring on the abuse to "get it over with."

In the second phase, a variety of abusive forms are expressed, depending on the situation and the couple. It could be physical abuse, emotional abuse, controlling behavior, or verbal abuse, like putting down and belittling.

Then in the third phase, the honeymoon phase, the abuser will come up with excuses for his or her act, or may deny that s/he did the act of abuse, may blame the victim for the abuse, or may blame others. There are lots of broken promises and some kindness to overcome the negative feelings and to "make up." So, now let's see if you understand this because I want to see how you can relate it to your situation. Also, this honeymoon phase is what is manifested when the couple is with others. Most of the time, friends and family don't see the abuse, control, or manipulation.

Sara: This is exactly my situation. With me, how it went was that his control/manipulation, or even abuse, were, as you called it, subtle or covert. Sometimes, I was able to put my finger on it, like when, at a party, he flirted with a woman. I complained to him and left the party. In the car, we got into a bit argument, and then he punched my mouth. I remember that I wore a white coat, and there was blood. I remember that he didn't feel any remorse. He said that it was my fault, and that he didn't punch me, but that I'm an "easy bleeder."

I remember a number of times when I was abused by him, I mean physically. But then, there were times that I was extremely frustrated by him, but couldn't point a finger at what was happening. I mean, I could see what was happening, but it just didn't measure up to my level of frustration with him. You know what I mean?

Therapist: Yes, this might be due to your ex-husband's passive-aggressive acts. Someone whose aggression comes out in indirect ways, a passive-aggressive person, may agree to do things for others, but doesn't follow through, and sometimes acts out annoying behavior while not consciously knowing its impact on others. A passive-aggressive person often feels put upon, controlled, pressured, and victimized. S/he is also frequently involved in fibbing, omitting information, or lying to avoid direct confrontation. Such person is in a deep state of denial, blaming everyone but himself for his behavior. There are many other symptoms, including an attempt to block or frustrate others with underlying anger, to plan to seed conflict between others, and gossiping, to signal mixed messages, manipulative behaviors etc.

Sara: I really had it hard with him, but on the other hand I was trying to keep everything inside, pretending that everything was more than okay. Even when I married him, everyone was surprised because they all thought I was way too good for him, or what we were a mismatch in almost every aspect, but I always defended him as my husband, and would take his side if someone wanted to put him down. I took his side and pretended that I was happy, so much and for so long, that when we got a divorce, many people who were not close to us were very shocked.

Therapist: That's very typical of abusive or dysfunctional relationships or situations. One thing I want to emphasize again is that abuse is not just physical abuse. There are emotional abuses, like neglect, controlling behaviors, and obsessions. All are harmful to the person who is the target. With your personality and your upbringing, you were trying to do the best you could by protecting what you thought, at that time, were your family's values. You wanted others to respect and value your husband, even if you didn't feel a sense of connection with him. It was because he was a part of your life, and you felt responsible for protecting him against an outsider. That's not uncommon. You may also have felt that if someone put down your husband, that s/he was putting you down, too, because, after all, you did marry him. Now, I do understand that you married him because you, in a way, had to. But, what I'm talking about here is what may be happening to you internally. Now, tell me, how much of this made sense?

Sara: All of it. I did feel like devaluing my husband was devaluing me. I find myself defending my family members if someone else wants to take advantage of them, even if that family member is not someone I feel close to. For example, my older brother, who I'm not close to because some of the habits and behaviors he has are just unbearable to me, because I think he is so damaging to himself, and as a result to his surroundings, and there's nothing I can do to help him. He always frustrated me, so I decided to stop talking to him until he got his act together, which of course did not happen, and he got worse over time. You know, what's amazing, my dad always wanted to help this brother more than any other of us. It seems like my father always rewards those with the worst behaviors. I was a good daughter to him, with the least trouble, and the one that brought him the most pride; but he always expected more from me.

Therapist: Sara, I can't help but wonder where your mom is in all of this. It seems to me that you've buried her somewhere, and are not thinking about her.

Sara: I guess you're right. I don't know where my mom is in my mind. She's definitely there, but I'm not quite sure where. But I think I explained that when it came to my parents, I remember a seemingly loveless marriage in which I hardly ever remember them having a healthy communication or expressing love to each other. I remember many fights, some of which were scary. My mom was very cold toward my dad, and my dad was always craving her love. Since he didn't get it, he would get angry.

Of course, my mom had her own reasons for not giving him the love he needed, but I think they fed each other's unhealthy relationship toward each other. My mom didn't show us that much love and affection, either. On the other hand, I do remember a lot of good family times, weekends with a lot of family members going to picnics, having a privileged material life compared to others around us, and having maids and servants taking care of us. I remember that both my parents were respected among their peers and colleges. I want to stop and see your view.

Therapist: As you're talking, I'm learning more about your family's system, because a family is, after all, a system composed of subsystems, and if one is able to learn its laws and follow them, then each individual within that family is able to be nurtured in a healthy environment, which is supposed to be the number one goal of a family.

In the family, the executive subsystem is that of the parents, and the sibling subsystem is that of the children. Invisible boundaries are the unspoken rules about who does what with whom, which are put around each member of the family so that each subsystem (or individual) can carry out his/her role to have a part in stabilizing the family tasks, while still staying connected to other members of the family.

One of the most common family problems is a weak

boundary between subsystems. An example would be a mother who calls too many times to check on her teenage son, to see if turned in his homework, or a husband who calls his mother every time he has a fight with his wife. These examples show an unhealthy and weak boundary between the immediate and the extended family. A family is seen more in a wholeness kind of a way, meaning that the system is greater than sum of the parts. A family is also a system in which each part affects all others in one way or another. In many cases, a dysfunctional family member controls the whole family with his behavior. His unavailability, abuse, controlling behaviors, and neglect of the family will affect interactions between each member of the family with any other. In these cases, the whole family learns to adapt, or it's better if we call it maladapt, itself to this member's behaviors.

A dysfunctional family member generally means a destabilizing family system. Therefore, for example, a passive-aggressive and controlling husband, who is not able to show love and communicate his feelings, and who is abusive at times toward his wife and children, in many cases, may be covered up by his wife. In an attempt to keep the family together, the wife will go to the extent of making up stories to cover up her husband's acts, or to show that they have a healthy marriage. She may even encourage her children to hide their true feelings and be dishonest to themselves. The wife may get depressed and anxious, not having enough energy or motivation to give affection to her children, causing some other blockages in their upbringing. Does it make sense so far?

Sara: Yes. So, for example, in my case, my ex-husband's behaviors could have caused me anxiety and sadness, and at times I did lose my motivation to focus on my children.

Since the divorce, my relationship with my children seems to be much healthier. It seems like I have so much more to give them, since I don't have to be focusing on their father's negative behaviors as much. I don't feel angry or anxious any more. I feel much calmer, and just altogether happier, and that, by itself, has caused my children to be happier. We have so many good times together. I've never seen any mother who has a better relationship with her children than I do. I mean, of course, I have disagreements, or normal mother/son tense moments; but we always manage to work through them.

Therapist: So, it seems like removing the member of the family who was causing the instability has helped the family in many ways. But what you should think about is that your ex-husband will always be a part of this family, directly or indirectly, and that you should try to figure out ways for your children to be connected to him without being damaged. I have this article that will give you information about this, Please feel free to take it home, read it and let me know if you have any questions. I want to say one more thing before we end today's session. To end the discussion of the family system, this system works best when subsystem boundaries are clear and balanced, meaning not too open and not too closed and rigid. When interactions are clear, authority figures are identified, rules are overt and flexible, and stressors and problems are confronted and communicated, rather than pushed away and denied. In such a family, members are clear about what to expect from one another, and neither intrude nor distance themselves, and there are open lines of communication. Each member in such a system feels comfortable and safe getting problems and hurt feelings out and talking about them and working on them rather than hiding away from them.

As the saying goes, "If there be righteousness in the heart, there will be beauty in the character. If there be beauty in the character, there will be harmony in the home. If there be harmony in the home, there will be order in the nation. If there be order in the nation, there will be peace in the world."

Unfortunately, in today's world most of us are unable to get that, and maybe that's a contributing factor to so much ignorance violence in the world. In addition to what we just talked about, I need you to pay attention to what I'm about to say for this week's work. Sometimes, we withhold our love from the people who have helped us the most, who may or may not be our parents. It's often the fact that with the help there was some hurt and rough times, too.

Then we start labeling them with words like "dysfunctional," or we think that they were abusive, emotionally or physically. Then we start to see them as the labels we put on them, not as individuals who are a combination of many different elements. Then we find ourselves starting to rewrite history, our memories start to change, and we start to only see one version of the story. When something goes outside the labeling we choose, our recollection of the memories fades.

I need you to be careful of this while you're going through the self-discovery process. I need you to go through your childhood memories, but try to see it as it was. For example, looking at the happy times and the pictures from those times, or talking about the good times you had, would give you a balanced view of reality. This way, the process of forgiveness will be easier to accomplish.

Now, one point is that some parents really are abusive, all the time. But most parents are just imperfect people who make mistakes. We don't want to blame anyone, we want to see the root of the problem and try to process it. Blaming others and yourself for problems only adds to frustration, which is not helpful for anyone and does not help with processing the issues. Does it make sense?

Sara: It makes great sense. I went through that, too. At the beginning of my divorce, I felt this extreme anger at my parents for letting me marry as if they were going to buy a pair of shoes. I mean, that's how much time and effort they put into it. I was mad that they didn't care. But the more I started talking about it, and the more I see it from a reasonable perspective, the more I'm able to see where that was coming from.

Perhaps, they just didn't know any better.

So, I'm not angry at them anymore. I just want to make sure I don't allow them to repeat the same mistakes when it comes to me. For example, I still see my mom wanting to tell me what to do, and the things she talks about that I don't even agree with. She gets so bossy and controlling at times. I constantly communicate with her that I don't welcome this type of behavior, and if she wants to spend time with me she has to make sure I enjoy it as much as she does, or that I will do less of that. I do the same with my dad.

Therapist: That's a great way to go. In a way, you're respecting your boundaries and letting other know that. That's an example of assertiveness. Now, I want you to think about it and we will talk about this more. How are you feeling now?

Sara: I feel great. There is a certain power in knowing. It seems like the more I learn about myself and how things are flowing around me, the more comfortable I feel about life overall.

We ended this session with a discussion of this week's homework for Sara. The homework gave Sara an example of her family's environment, in which her mom and dad were fighting a lot. In this family, the daughter, Sara, has learned that she can make things better in the household if she's good in every aspect and pleases mom and dad when they're about to argue. By Sara putting forth some control over her home environment; by being a perfect daughter, she is able to avoid physical or emotional abuse from her parents because of her complaints.

In this homework, we also identified the word homeostasis.

Homeostasis is defined as equilibrium, or a sense of balance, in the family. Unless the family addresses their problems, the children will surely be affected by any dysfunctional pattern of behavior. For example, Sara's adult life may be characterized as a constant attempt to please others in order to gain their approval or to avoid conflict. She may try to look to others as they expect her to, and be what they want her to be rather than being her true self. These, if not addressed and processed, can affect her adult life and future relationships, as well as her full emotional/mental/spiritual growth.

Sara's homework was to think about this and write as many examples as she felt comfortable with, but at the same time, to relax herself whenever she felt overwhelmed.

Session 6

The following session we started after a little small talk and me asking Sara how her week was.

Sara: My week was a week full of adventure. I can tell you that my life is not boring anymore. This path of self discovery is quiet a journey. As I get deeper into it, I become more captivated and amazed by the whole process, and how I have been so ignorant of it. It seems like I've woken up. It seems like I've opened my baggage and am letting go of the waste, one at a time. It's amazing how I used to not know that what I was carrying was waste.

It also seems like I'm wiping the dust of the mirror of my true inner being. I also feel so sad when I see so many people who are totally unaware of themselves and their lives, and what it really means. It seems to be that there are so many lost souls, confused, overwhelmed, and not taking even one step to make things better. As I get more information and apply it to myself and my life, I feel emotionally expanded. I don't know how else to explain it. I really do feel like my mind is expanding, and now I'm learning what it means when they say, think outside the box, even though many who say it don't practice what they preach, because they're just imitating what others are saying. They don't really know what it means.

As I thought about my childhood, how I tried to be the perfect girl, how I was very compliant, how I pretended and lost my true self in the process, how I ended up making the wrong decision when I wanted to get married, how it affected my life and led my life to where I am now, how I idealize people, wrongly, how I saw things superficially. And how many of the very downsides of my life turned out to be, in some ways, positive experiences, because I chose them to be positive.

Instead of turning toward negative behaviors and loosing hope, I decided to turn to positive behaviors, like seeking therapy to discover myself, drawing, writing, doing well at my job, and, most important being a better mother, besides doing a lot charity work, which helps me see the bigger picture of life.

Just thinking more about it makes me more aware of my role in all of it, and what improvements I need to make, instead of blaming others. Blaming others doesn't really help much, except cause anger and frustration in me. I can't change others. Instead of focusing on finding shortcomings in others, I've learned, or should say that I'm learning, to shift my focus on myself and what I could do to not get into that situation anymore.

What is this blaming others? I used to do it a little bit, but my ex-husband was the master of it. He blamed everyone else for everything, never himself. He never turned the camera on his own deficiencies. For example, our divorce was because of my family, my friends, my co-workers, my spiritual beliefs, my education. You name it, he said it. Never once did he say, "Wait a minute, maybe I was a part of this."

Where does this come from, I mean to this extreme?

Therapist: There are a combination of reasons for people who blame others for their problems. The personal factors that are related to the likelihood that other-blame will occur include the person's inability to find the good or benefit in a bad situation. That ability is characterized by statements like, "Maybe it's for the better," and "Some good may come out of this."

Similarly, people who tend to make downward comparisons, like, "I'm fortunate for what I have. Others have lost so much more," are less likely to blame others.

The other factor is the person's attribution style. Some people tend to find fault with others in many situations, regardless of the circumstances. No matter how illogical the rationale, some people cling to the need to blame others for everything bad that happens to them. In contrast, other people have an attribution style which leads to a tendency to blame themselves, no matter how obviously blameworthy someone else is. There should be no blame at all, not to self and not to others. A mistake should be analyzed and processed in order to be able to move on. So, let's go back to your experience, what else comes to your mind?

Sara: I can see that, like any other human being, I'm a combination of unlimited factors, and that I have so much power to change my way of being and my way of life by the way I think and respond to situations. It's all making sense now. In a way, things are becoming more clear. I find myself very much more selective as to how and with whom I want to spend my time. I'm trying hard not to waste it, and get the most from each day. My dream is to learn something new every day, because I've come to realize that the more I learn, the less I become biased, prejudiced, and racist. I understand now what it means when they say that ignorance is the root of discrimination against others, based on first impression factors. I mean, I still have preferences, but I'm starting not to look at things as good or bad, but as similar and different. I know I'm jumping all over the place. It feels like I want to share with you all the changes that are happening in my level of awareness. I feel like I'm in the process of change, not finished with it. You know what I mean?

Therapist: Yes, I do. All the feelings you say you have, related to this experience, are normal. There're a combination of excitement, sadness, happiness, joy, surprise, anger, and many other feelings, both positive and negative. You have to make sure you let these feelings express themselves, acknowledge them, analyze them, and process them.

Feelings are signals for us to pay attention to our empty spots. These empty spots need to be filled when one is walking through the process of self-discovery. The more we learn about our identity, who we are, our blockages and what caused them, our weaknesses, our strengths, and how each factor in our environment played a part in who we are, the more we're able to learn about our true self; our strengths, our weaknesses, our uniqueness, our talents, and our limitations. In this process, we have to constantly challenge our irrational ways of thinking and replace them with rational ones. Each one of us has a set of subconscious general rules for living that determine how we interact with life. Some of these rules may be based on irrational patterns of thinking that may have been functional for our ancestors, but are not functional for us, any more, but we never took time to look into them, analyze them, and see what they're based on. Imitation is easier than learning new things and changing, so some of us just imitate others. Life is evolving, and with it educational tools, religion, science, etc. It should be evolving, or there will be a conflict. We never took the time to see whether these beliefs, which used to be functional at one point, are still functional for our life, today. As a result, these ways of thinking may end up hurting us. One has to start analyzing these thoughts, based on facts, and on what these thoughts have done to the person's life. Have they been a productive part of his or her life, or a blockage for growth? Which ones do they need to hold on to, and which do they have to let go of? Now, can you think of a couple of examples of these patterns of thinking that may have damaged you, one way or the other?

Sara: Maybe, for example, the thought that "in order for me to be good enough, I must be good at everything I do, I must be better than everyone else, I must keep my dad proud at all levels and at all costs." Or some of my religious beliefs like, "If you do this, you will go to hell," imposing a lot of guilt and fear.

Therapist: That's good. Let's focus on the first one for now, and discuss the second one later. Think about what this pattern of thinking, which you now know is irrational, because nobody can be better than others at all levels of life, did to you and to your life.

Sara: I didn't react to my unhappy marriage. I didn't tell others about my unhappy marriage, because that would mean I wasn't successful at making it work. It would also be a source of shame to my dad. The ideal girl image that my dad had of me would be tarnished.

Therapist: Good insight. So, we have these set of "rules for living," and in some cases, many of them may be irrational. Rules are underlying beliefs that lead us through our reaction to life. How we evaluate specific events that happen to us depends on these underlying subconscious or automatic thinking patterns. There are some core beliefs that need to change, because they cause unhelpful emotions and behaviors in you. In your case, you had this rule of being an "ideal girl" that was not reasonable, meaning that, based on facts and reason, there is no such a thing. What does 'ideal' mean in a world that's constantly changing and evolving? A person is supposed to be constantly changing and developing physically, emotionally, mentally, and spiritually. How can one define words like perfect and ideal in such states of being? We could say we're walking toward our whole self, meaning that we're experiencing every piece of who we are in the process of self-knowledge, but there is no such thing as perfect. Anybody who looks for this is limiting her self. Now, tell me what other beliefs do you think were damaging to you, that need to change?

Sara: "I must please everyone," would be one, I think. "I must not make any mistakes in my life," would be another. Um…I can't think of another one now. Maybe you can help me. Uh, "What if others misunderstand this? What if they judge me?"

Therapist: That's good. So, what would a thought like, "I must not make any mistakes in my life," do to a person? Is it possible not to make any mistakes?

Sara: Not really.

Therapist: That's right. Mistakes are part of life. If one is not making mistakes, it could mean that she isn't doing much with her or his life. We learn from mistakes and move on. The point is not to make no mistakes but not to make the same one twice. Now, when one has learned, in her childhood, to feel guilty or ashamed for making mistakes, she learns to hide from challenges because of the possibility of making mistakes.

This could be referred back to your previous statement, where, as a part of your irrational thinking, you reported that you said to yourself something like, if you do this you will go to hell. This hell is our own creation; a creation where its participants act out of fear rather than from learning and love. A psychologist may explain hell as a person's emotional ups and downs, impulsivity, and lack of control of her life and surroundings. These types of thinking patterns may result in the person having a lot of fear of moving forward in her life and growing, because she is constantly asking herself, "What if I make a mistake?"

This fear of making a mistake and feeling the guilt that she learned to feel as a child, and also the fear of "hell," may block her from the true sense of "heaven," which is a fully expanded mind; an inner peace that results from learning to accept. Some of the other ways of irrational thinking I could see that may exist in you might be, "I need love and approval from others, and I must avoid disapproval from any source."

This could lead to you being dishonest with yourself, and sacrificing your own needs, beliefs, and, in a way, your being, to get other people's approval. This, as you've reported, may not be working for you. Everyone is a unique individual, and has the basic right of choosing what works for her. Tell me what you think.

Sara: I felt anxious for a large portion of my life. I felt like I was lost and couldn't feel the meaning of my life. I mean, I did have happy and exciting moments, but my life didn't have a meaning. I was just being, but not living. I had not found who I truly was. I started to live in a mask that was not the truth, and I, myself, started to believe it.

Therapist: When one experiences some forms of anxiety, other forms of thinking that may be a part of her, and which she has to divest herself from, are, "In order to be a worthwhile person, I must achieve and be successful at whatever I do, and make no mistakes," or "Everyone must love me," or that, "I need to please everyone I love at all times."

These forms of unreasonable expectations pressure one into trying to reach a goal that's impossible and useless. She's created it, but it isn't real. Every time we walk toward something unreal, we're digging into a troublesome hole, deeper and deeper. Usually, what ends up happening when we have these sorts of unreasonable ways of thinking that have a lot of words like should, must, have to, always, and everyone, we lose motivation and end up not reaching even our own potential, let alone something higher than that.

Another way to put this is to frame it into what we call "people pleasers." Everyone knows and has heard that it's good to be a pleasant individual, but also, like everything else, the whole point is learning to be balanced. Being pleasant is different from a people pleaser. Too much kindness, helpfulness, and submission are common among people who have certain patterns of irrational thinking. Then comes the unhealthy pattern of being a "people pleaser," which can be explained as the tendency to supply for others at the cost of personal well-being, both mentally and physically. This pattern of living allows others to manipulate, be insensitive, or take advantage of the people pleaser, leaving such a person with resentment, anger, anxiety, or depression. People pleasers have a number of characteristics, which include the need to be accountable for what is not theirs.

For example, a woman who sees her husband's neglectful behavior as a sign of her shortcomings, and becomes insecure, needs to work on her pattern of thinking.

Somehow, during their childhood upbringing, people pleasers have learned that they're responsible for other people's moods and behaviors, and are carrying this dirty baggage of thinking with them throughout life.

The second characteristic is that people pleasers, sometimes, go with the other person's unreasonable demands to avoid conflict. They may go along with manipulators, controllers, abusers, and selfishness. By avoiding their responsibility as a person who needs to stand up for their rights, they're contributing to the other person's bad habits.

Another characteristic of people pleasers is that they

deny what's healthy, and usually engage in damaging relationships because they don't want to accept reality. The reality is that people pleasers don't want to be bothered with the extra effort needed to walk out of a damaging environment and take steps to make it healthy. They use the denial mechanism as a tool, and label their kindness or helpfulness as a good trait, instead of looking for escape tools. Finally, people pleasers have no knowledge of who they are, what they want, and what meaning their life has. They live according to other people's needs and wants, and don't know how to respect themselves. Does it make sense to you?

Sara: Yes, it does make sense. When I try to make everyone love me, it means that I'm probably being untruthful in some way or other. That even goes against the law of attraction, which says likes attract. It doesn't mean that one is bad or good, it just means that when we have certain values and ways of life, we're automatically more drawn and attracted toward similar people. A person who attracts and pleases everyone could probably be categorized as someone who molds into other peoples' way of thinking and set of values. That means that this person does not have a formed identity. Am I right?

Therapist: You explained it well. A person who gets to know herself, who has a well-balanced self-esteem, and who discovers herself, needs to have a certain set of rules and values that go hand in hand with who she is. As a result, she goes with her genuine and honest self, rather than pretending to be something else.

It's the same with most anything else in life. Let's say, for example, if you want to get a high level of education, can you afford to hang out with a group of partying people who want to go clubbing every night and give you the temptation for it? Or, do you hang out with a group that has the same goals of studying and working hard to get where they want to get? Of course, you won't choose the first group, or if you do, then that means that your intention, which is wanting to achieve higher education, and which needs hours of dedication to studying and planning, is not in accordance and harmony with your behavior, which is going to places and hanging out with people who encourage otherwise.

And that, by itself, means turmoil.

Our intention, meaning, and goals in life, what we want to do, and who we want to be should become clear to us and be in agreement with how we behave toward those intentions. Now, let's see, I need to ask you what changes you've been able to implement in these ways of thinking, referring to the ones you discussed, and what you see happening as a result

Sara: Well, I should tell you that I'm seeing a lot of changes. I was reading about self-knowledge and Carl Jung; about the concept of self-actualization. I wanted to talk to you about it, related to myself. I also read that only 2% of people are actually able to get to be self-actualized.

Therapist: Some psychologists believe, based on the characteristics and research, that only a small portion of the population actually gets to the top of the pyramid of self-actualization and self-growth, not because they can't get there, but because they get stuck fulfilling their more primitive and animalistic needs rather than the higher ones. The need for self-actualization is one of the highest needs of every human. We lose this concept, somewhere in the process of life, because we are not focusing on it.

Sara: What I read explained self-actualization as those people who see reality and facts. Rather than rejecting the truth, these people have high peak experiences, and are tolerant of themselves and others. This, by itself, is self-explanatory, and I hardly know of anyone, in my personal life, who has reached this level. I know of many people who think they are self-actualized, but the funny thing is that they're actually among the least self-actualized. Why is that?

Therapist: Well, like anything else, there could be multiple reasons. The lower our level of awareness of ourselves and our surroundings, the more we fall into denial of the truth. On the other hand, the more we learn and educate ourselves about the truth, by learning about ourselves, nature, and science, and the more we become knowledgeable and practice what we learn, the more we come to realize how unlimited this world and its content is, and how little we truly know. When we come to realize this, our level of judging others will decrease, and we'll become more tolerant of others, as well as of life's shortcomings. What this means is that we will accept reality as it throws itself at us.

Now, some people think this means not doing anything and waiting to see what comes at us. On the other hand, what it means is to do the best we can, at all levels of life, to get the most of it, because we are given one life to live, and remember that the goal is to realize this Self. Self-actualization is considered to be a more mature way of comprehending life as it unfolds. Self-actualized individuals seem to have a sense of purpose for life, genuine interpersonal relationships that are meaningful in quality, consequential activities, logical ways of thinking, the ability to identify with higher human values, and self respect. So, do you think you're getting close to this level?

Sara: I certainly think that I'm more honest to myself, and as a result am more genuine in my relationships. What I mean by this is that if I don't like someone's behavior I don't pretend otherwise. I'm not disrespectful to them, but I feel more comfortable hanging out with people who share the same interests and values. I'm more goal-oriented; goals that are based on what I like, not what others expect of me. My activities are much more quality-oriented rather than an attempt to get quantity. I am definitely more logical when it comes to making decisions. I still get emotional sometimes, and want to react, but I'm learning more and more to stop and think, based on reason. This has been greatly affecting me and my life, in so many ways. I'm more detrimental than ever to walk through life the way I choose. I guess I'm more in tune with my higher parts of the self. You know?

Therapist: Sure. People who start to function at the self-actualized level move beyond ego-oriented needs. They identify more with their sense of higher self. What other changes are you noticing?

Sara: I'm trying to focus more on the present, but, as you said, I'm trying to process the past, too. This was a great learning experience for me. By thinking about my childhood memories, I was able to move out of idealizing my father, seeing reality as it was, acknowledging the good as well as the bad times, processing them, learning about them and what effects they had on my sense of self, processing them, and then accepting them and moving on.

This has made me into a totally different person.

These changes are coming very rapidly. I feel like I'm turning into a new person. When I look at the past, I remember my dad a lot, I think because I had the most conflict with him during my recent changes, including my divorce. But I remember many memories of him that tell me he loved me. I remember how proud he was of me and my education, and the fact that I was a good mother, a good housewife, and at the same time a good student. I remember that he was always showing me off, talking about how I was good at everything and able to manage things in a balanced way. Him kissing me every day, and if he didn't have a kiss one day, he would say, "Where are my beautiful daughter and her pleasant kisses?" I remember when he went on trips. I was the one getting the most presents. I still see his old beliefs, for example that he sees assertiveness in woman as aggressiveness. There's no middle ground between the two for him, when it comes to women. I've learned to accept that, and have clear boundaries with him. That's the only way I can have a reasonably healthy relationship with him, with clear boundaries of respect for both me and him. Deep down inside, I will always love him, and I will pray for him to be able to get out of the state he's in and move up. He's certainly capable of it. I want the best for him, but there's not much I can do at this point to truly help him. If he ever wants to make changes and asks me for help, I'll rush to it, but I don't think it will ever happen.

Therapist: You will feel yourself more attentive to how your life is unfolding and how it's evolving toward a purposeful life. Remember what we discussed. Self-actualized people tend to have inner-directed, independent, and self-supportive behaviors, and they seem to have less need for approval from other people. This, however, does not mean that they don't care about other people. On the other hand, they're the most productive people of their society. They benefit their surroundings, rather than take advantage of them. They're the ones who not only do not harm others and the world, but also benefit both. They make their decisions based on their own core of consciousness. Okay now, I have to let you know that our time is about over and I want you to relax while I give you this week's homework.

At the end of this session, Sara relaxed and we reviewed the work she was supposed to do. She seemed calm and excited.

Session 7

The following session, Sara came in looking different. Every time, she brings in a slightly different person. This time she was a very quiet Sara, but seemed calm and relaxed. We started the session after a little small talk.

> **Therapist:** So, tell me how your week was, and what went on with you, your feelings, your thoughts, and your life altogether.

> **Sara:** Well, I went through the homework. I did remember a lot of positive things about my life, in general. We had many family vacations that were fun. My dad used to make a lot of money, before he went bankrupt. During that time, we had a luxurious life. We had servants and many parties. I remember having some fun times with my cousins.

> This homework was good, because it reminded me of the many good times we had together. So, it gave me a sense of balance. With my brothers, I do remember that

they loved me in their own way. I couldn't come up with specific examples, but I know they just can't comprehend the difficulty I'm in right now, or they would have helped more. I think that, in a way, means that I have forgiven them. I don't think I'm in denial, because the way I react is the way I feel. But why does it matter so much that my brothers didn't help me during this period? It makes sense that it's painful. Then I remembered that I don't really need their help, that this is a path I have to walk by myself, and that this is a mess I have to get out of by myself, with hope and determination. I can choose to see what makes me comfortable, and deal with them that way. I don't have to pretend to be too close to them while my heart feels otherwise.

I will be true to myself, and that's the best gift I can give myself. The more I do that, the less resentment I have toward them. Even though I don't see them often, and don't talk to them much, deep down in my heart I want the best for them and their families. I want them to grow, to discover themselves. If they're ready to do that and ask me for help, I would help them. But until they're ready, I will let them go. This is better for everyone, or at least, this is what I think, right now. I know now that nobody is obligated to help another if they aren't ready to do so, just like nobody is obligated to be in constant contact with those she doesn't feel comfortable with, even if they're her family members.

All the changes I started to make as a woman, becoming more assertive, standing up for my rights, demanding respect or else; all these were perhaps seen by them as wanting too much, and having high expectations. Maybe what they're used to is women being happy with having their basic needs met.

Therapist: There are signs to let us know whether a relationship is unhealthy. When these signs are present, the worst thing we can do to ourselves is to let it stay the way it is, without taking any action to either "fix it or release it."

There's a point where we have to get from the point of wondering what to do and self-pity, and move toward taking action. There are long-term consequences to negative relationships. Every relationship needs a reasonable level of stability and compatibility. Sometimes the dynamics of the individual's interaction needs to change. In your diaries, I read the word "back-stabbing" a number of times. Having this inner feeling, and continuing to have a relationship, as if nothing has happened, with those you think are behaving in ways you consider back-stabbing would be very questionable, and can cause intense conflict and anxiety in you.

What you did was perhaps the best way to go. You decided a number of times to explain to them, and when you felt like they just did not want to understand, you decided to stop talking to them until you were ready. Or, I should say, until *they* were ready to understand that this is your life, and that they have no right to make decisions for you, and that what they were doing was a selfish act rather than a helpful one. If they are not able to comprehend this fact, then how you want to react is totally up to you. Whether you want to start a relationship with clear boundaries, to make sure they don't cross and disrespect your boundaries, like before, or just decreasing the friction alltogether and minimizing your communication with them; this is totally *your* choice, and no one has the right to tell you what to do.

There is no one right way. There is only what works. You go with your inner feelings and your inner heart. The same goes with every situation; a cheating/controlling husband, a parent who neglects her child and is in complete denial over it, and expresses complete surprise about her estranged relationship with the child when she grows up, a friend who has two faces, a co-worker who lies. These are all examples of bad relationships people may have.

It's a totally personal decision about how one wants to deal with a "bad" relationship. For a person who wants to make it better, there are two ways; either to take steps to change the dynamics of the relationship to make it better, or to move out and on with her life. The fact one has to pay attention to is that if one doesn't take any action and lets the unhealthy relationship be as it is, there are serious long-term consequences. One example would be a wearing away of self-worth. Suddenly, the only identity the person has is the one imposed by her abuser, controller, or neglector. She sees herself through their eyes. This person may even suffer from serious personality disorders.

Another damaging effect would be this person's inability to accept the love of another person who is well-intentioned. S/he becomes suspicious of the other's sincerity, leading to undermining the possibility of future positive relationships. This person subconsciously expects the same treatment from others, making it difficult for her/him to engage in a healthy relationship in which there is genuine love and acceptance.

A relationship is unhealthy if one person feels afraid of the other, feels controlled or unable to express true feelings and thoughts, feels happier when this person is not around, wants to get out but don't want to be lonely, or feels small or inadequate. If the answer to any of these questions is yes, it means that you are probably in a dysfunctional relationship and need to make a decision about what you want to do, or if you want to continue with it. It might be time to do an evaluation of the benefits you get from it, versus the harms it imposes upon you. If the second outweighs the first, it's time to take some serious action for change. No one can do this for you except yourself.

One might ask, "Now that I'm aware that my relationship is dysfunctional, now what?" Well, there are two ways to go about this. One is an instant decision to end the relationship, which will only work if one has had time to plan the course of action, and has the means and support needed to go with the plan.

This decision depends on the severity of the situation and the type of relationship. The person may be ready for the sudden changes, and has made sure that this is the only and the best way out of the relationship, by investigating it thoroughly, thinking it through, and being sure about it. One also needs to process any unreasonable level of guilt for getting out of the relationship. This guilt may be associated with the low sense of self-worth that the relationship has imposed upon her/him.

However, in many other cases, we don't need to make such a sudden and drastic change and move. We can learn about and recognize the strengths we know we have, and let others treat us as we see ourselves deserve to be treated, so there is no need to separate ourselves. Having clear boundaries is the best way to go. We identify our boundaries, clearly communicate them to the other we want to have a relationship with, or continue our relationship with, and we make sure those boundaries are respected. We have to have a course of action planned and ready, ahead of time, if these boundaries are broken, and at the same time make sure we do the same to the other person, meaning that we respect their boundaries, too. After all, we have to practice what we preach. This will increase the chances of us saving a relationship that still has a chance.

At this point, Sara looked tired, so I encouraged her to relax and take a break. She seemed to be thinking very deeply about what she had gone through during therapy. While she was taking a sip out of her cup, looking at her, I couldn't help but think, How can an intelligent, beautiful, and accomplished woman stay in a marriage like this for such a long time? Why did she not get out of it?

And then I remembered her story, her family's pattern of thinking toward her being the ideal girl who would never do anything to harm the family, including getting a divorce, which is not very accepted in the family, the way she wanted and thought she had to make everything work, at any cost, even the cost of her own emotional wellness.

But why?

Most such behaviors are due to irrational patterns of thinking, fear and anxiety of change, low self-worth, and insecurities; thinking that the change may not make things better. After I felt she was ready to start the process, I did so.

Therapist: You know Sara, to continue with what I was saying, there are many ways to go about ending or solving an unhealthy relationship. Divorce is not the only answer, but it is one when there is no other solution. In your situation, it seems like the best solution was to get a divorce and it's something that you not only don't regret, but enjoy.

But, one has to consider the important factor that many families, when faced with a stressful situation, choose divorce as a way to distance themselves from the problems caused by a dysfunctional system. While this is a common way for dealing with what seem to be irreconcilable problems, unless the parties involved in the divorce resolve their own contributions to the failed relationship, there is strong likelihood that old and destructive behaviors will re-surface in later relationships. There is an old saying that goes like this: You can divorce your spouse, but you can never divorce yourself. Unresolved dysfunctional behavior patterns are easily transferred to new relationships.

Humans tend to take their familiar role in one family system and repeat that role in other systems they enter. However, there are other people who choose not to do anything about the problems and just stay with them, not being proactive. But, one has to consider that any dysfunctional family pattern leaves scars on the members of the system, including the children. The matter that's very important is that the system's view does not blame the family's problems on a given family member. With accurate identification of the process that sustains painful or stressful conditions in the family, change for the better can be both profound and permanent. Does it make sense so far?

Sara: Yes, but can you relate this to my situation?

Therapist: Sure. That's exactly what I was about to do. In your case, you took the role of the giver. You took whatever came at you, and that's why you got more of it coming, only in different ways. You didn't demand more. You, as a member of the family, were trying to, as you word it, please your dad and your family. You cared more about what others think than about your own well-being. So, you made a choice not to make a change.

I'm not saying you could have fixed your ex-husband and his abusive, manipulative, and controlling behavior, which seem to have been a result of his insecurities and his inattentiveness to his adult side. I'm not saying that anything could have helped you love him more, since it's obvious that you had no affection for him and didn't feel attracted to him on any level. I'm just saying you could have chosen to come up with a way out of the situation sooner.

See, when someone looks at herself when a problem comes, it gets easier to focus on the solution rather than the problem. When one focuses on the problem, one gets angry, resentful, and frustrated, and phrases like, "why me?" "what if?" and all sort of things go though one's mind. But when one is willing to see her role in a situation, and see it as a give-and-take sort of a thing, then one is able to learn from it and use it to foster growth in herself; not repeating the same patterns, and not letting herself get in the same situation.

Then the experience has not been lost, and she has gained knowledge from it. That's when one looks back and sees every experience in a more positive light. Another subject that seems relevant to discuss here is why we marry who we marry. In your case, your partner was chosen for you, so you didn't have much control over it, but the fact that you stayed in this relationship may be, somehow, related to what I'm about to discuss about partnership and who we pick.

One theory states that some of us marry the worst parts of our parents. If that's the case, then maybe this unique opportunity of having conflicts that are similar to our childhood conflicts can help us finish that unfinished business, but this time with better equipment. When you experience an emotionally distant father, and then find yourself in the same situation with your husband, anxiety or depression may overcome you. But, as an adult, rather than as a dependent child, some people may be able to have a more productive relationship. On the other hand, another version of the story is that one may be attracted to those precisely opposite to one's parents as a way of avoiding the difficulties of those early relationships. A person who is looking for a healthy relationship should be aware of these facts to be able to choose a middle ground between the two situations. Differences in a relationship can expand one's range and help in the balancing-out process. Therefore, up to a point, and depending on what the difference is, and how it's dealt with, it may even be healthy. After all, we all think that our way is the normal way, because we're so used to it, but when someone else comes into the picture we have to learn new ways, and that's where compromise comes into play.

A relationship in which both partners respect each other's independence and autonomy while wanting to be emotionally, physically, and spiritually close to each other is one that benefits each party. Harmony is the number one key for a relationship, *any* relationship. Harmony means being in accordance and in agreement with one another, and respecting each other's differences. Another key is to learn about these factors and our own needs and personality, and to gain knowledge. Another way to explain the controlling or abusing behavior, and why people stay for so long in such relationships, is that there are many people who stay in bad relationships, and there's a good explanation why that happens. These individuals don't think they deserve any better. In other words, they have a low sense of self-value. Therefore, self-esteem is a factor. Many of these people would feel better about themselves if they weren't in such a relationship. Having a feeling of being controlled, criticized, rejected, neglected, or abused, drags them down and takes from them the strength needed to take an action.

There's more to the story, though. These people become painfully bonded with the damaging person. This painful bond is imposed by pain, and causes an unhealthy attachment rather than a healthy connection. Sometimes, the more traumatic the bond, the harder it is to get out. It's like they get used to the pain, and it becomes something of an addiction. The addict knows that the drug is destroying her, but uses it anyhow. She doesn't know why, but keeps on doing it. Another fact that increases this hurtful bond is that the abuser or controller, every once in a while, will give the abused, or the person who is the victim, something nice and rewarding. For a person with low self-esteem, that would be a lot, and something to make them hang in there. Does it make sense?

Sara: It makes perfect sense. I think my relationship lacked harmony and chemistry.

Therapist: Yes, that's right. Remember, some of the main blockages of self-actualization are fear of challenge, irrational beliefs, and lack of knowledge about the self and surroundings. Can you give me some examples related to your situation with each of these?

Sara: Fear of what others might think if I do this, or if I do that. Fear of what if people close to me reject me for doing this. Fear of what if people judge me. Irrational thinking, an example would be me thinking that I should be perfect at everything I do, and even if I didn't feel that way, as long as people thought it, that would be good enough. The irrational belief that you go into a marriage until death do you part, no matter what the circumstances and what your feelings are toward the functionality of the marriage.

As an example of lack of knowledge, there are many. I truly did not know who I was. I always knew I had much good in me, but was so over-involved with trying to impress others that I never got a chance to use the strengths I had. Doctor, I know this may not be directly related, but I have a question about why people gossip.

Therapist: Well there are a number of reasons. Gossiping too   much could become an unhealthy habit instead of actually dealing with problems. One of the functions of gossip is supposed to be to help us begin to forget about our own problems, or see them in a more positive light when comparing it to others. If we see other people having problems too, then it normalizes the obstacles we're having in life. Most of us do it because it's become a habit, and because we enjoy putting others down by focusing on their problems, rather than seeing them as normal humans with a combination of weaknesses and strengths. When it comes to people in power, hearing about their problems humanizes them. They become real people, with whom others can identify. Therefore, a little bit of gossiping, if it doesn't become a habit and we know when to stop, and if it doesn't hurt the other person, may be normal functioning of human beings teaching us what the limits are, and also helping us forget about our own problems by knowing that others have the same.

Researchers report that almost everyone who lives a routine social life gossips in one way or another. Adults usually gossip to bring down someone they think has more power over them in some form or way,. That helps them feel better about themselves. One has to learn to be able to distinguish between facts, gossip, and rumors.

Gossip is always about people, and can be either factual or an assumption.

Rumors are always speculative, and have been called "a collective hypothesis." For one person, the rumor may look like the truth, but for the other it's the total opposite. Rumors are based on people's anxieties and uncertainties. Rumors are mostly a projection of the individual who started them. They reveal the desires and fears of the individual, and those who are attracted to that rumor. That's why it's easier to spread a rumor among those who have a lot of anxieties and unsure-ness. For example, it is easier to discuss a divorce, and spread a rumor about it, to an unhappy couple than to a happy one. The unhappy couple, due to their own uncertainties, and fears related to their relationship, project that to others and are attracted to a rumor when they see one, and may even contribute to the process of spreading it to others. These uncertainties and fears make the couple blind to the effects this rumor may have on the people who the gossip is about. In regard to your first discussion regarding your fear, it was very insightful. Again, remember that people who have been able to get to a more mature level of self-growth follow their own inner vision, have fewer needs and attachments, are not very concerned with results, have their own definition of what is productive for them, and are aware of their choices and the effect these choices have on them and the world. The more you know yourself, the more you become determined and hopeful, once you make a decision to finish it all the way.

Sara: Why is it that people who are emotionally more mature have less needs and attachments? This is what

I have from you, I actually wrote it here. People who are categorized as self-actualized have less basic needs and insecure attachments; it is a built-in system. As one matures more and more toward self-actualization, one becomes a more self-sufficient being. It's like mountain climbing. The higher you go, the harder it gets, but at the same time you're getting stronger to deal with the difficulties.

We all have needs as we grow up, but as we get into our adult life, depending on the level and intensity of self-discipline, we will be able to control these needs according to priorities and long-term benefits. If we categorize the self into three different levels of child, adult, and guidance, then it is the child self that corresponds to our body and feelings, is below our conscious awareness, and is the one that gives us signals when we have desires, pleasures, or feel pain and other physical forms of response. This level of child self is the one that learns to do physical things, and by repetition of the same thinking forms habits. One has to pay attention to this child self with kindness and patience, and then teach and discipline it, to train and mold it to support his or her intentions in life. This is the beginning of the process of self-control. As children, due to lack of necessary physical/emotional/ and mental tools, we need others to take care of us. Therefore, we form attachments. However, once we develop physically and mentally, and mature in all these aspects, we need to let go of these attachments and become more self sufficient. Then we can have a sense of healthy connection rather than attachment. For example, if my child self has needs, then it is my higher selves that should look into it and see how and whether the need should be met immediately. In other words, I should train myself to function from my higher state of being, the more mature one. Right?

Therapist: Yes, something of that nature. It also means we don't act impulsively. We think before we act, we find the best solutions by thinking about them, the most healthy ones, and those that don't have harmful long-term affects. It also means that we focus on the solution rather than the problem, and we do not make the problem bigger or smaller than it really is. Altogether, a person who is aiming to become self-actualized becomes a more rational human being, with a sense of meaning toward his/her life, and a balanced focus in all areas of his or her interest.

These kinds of people have a healthy sense of connection toward their surroundings, which can generate a sense of freedom and love for the people who encounter them. In their inner relationships, they have a symbiotic form of relationship, in which everyone feels like they are benefiting, instead of a feeling of being controlled or drained. The word "need" can be explained as a psychological trait that causes a person to move toward and take steps for reaching a goal, which guides him or her in having a sense of direction for the behavior that moves her or him forward. People have a wide variety of needs, ranging from basic to advanced, for example, from hunger to security, to self-actualization.

Some needs are more powerful than others. The lower forms of needs are similar to those of animals. However, only humans have higher needs. A person who is self-liberated is one who is free from insecure attachments and lower forms of excessive needs that lead to destructive behaviors. How are you?

Sara: Everything you say, I automatically related it to my situation and me. I see that my ex-husband thought that he loved me. However, it was not a form of love. I think he was benefiting from me, but I didn't feel like I was getting anything from him. Benefits in a marriage would go from financial or material to deeper forms of emotional, to the spiritual. I don't feel like I got any of that from my ex-husband. I mean, financially we were struggling for the majority of out marriage, until right before the divorce, when his job started to pick up, but at the same time he became more controlling and his behavior started to get even stranger. Emotionally, he didn't have the smallest clue as to how to deal with my needs. Spiritually, he was nowhere close to my beliefs, and I lost my motivation for a short while. He called obsessions, and insecure and anxious attachments, "love." If you asked him, he'd say we had a perfect marriage.

Can you explain the word love? I do want to find a man I love, and experience that true feeling, but I find myself unable to do so, at this point. I don't know whether I'm just scared, because of what my ex-husband has done to me, or that it's just hard for someone like me to find a true match. I think that I don't need a person financially. Emotionally and spiritually, I think I'm much stronger and have fewer needs. Therefore, sometimes I think, "Why risk it?" I'm starting to have a good life. I have wonderful children, a good job, and many other positive things that are going well for me. Do I really want to risk getting involved with another man? What if I get emotionally attracted to him and it doesn't work out? Another damage? Can I take that?

This is what I have from what you said. Love consists of three components: intimacy, commitment, and passion. A fruitful form of love is the one that forms a system in which everyone feels good and nurtured, and benefits from each other, and one in which everyone gives and receives in a natural flow. Here's where the word equivalent comes into play. When we say two people have to be each other's match for a healthy relationship, they complement each other's shortcomings, and one tunes in with the other.

On the other hand, another word for it is harmony. Harmony does not mean the exactly similar. A little bit of a difference makes the relationship better, because partners learn from each other. Harmony means being respectful and interested in each other's growth and values, and not being in opposition. Having values and interests in common is another aspect of harmony. What damages a relationship is two individuals who are in opposition to each other's personalities, needs, and maturity level.

A healthy form of relationship is a system in which its members can gain emotional, physical, and spiritual nurturing for development, instead of one member feeling blocked by the other member. This is why we can never judge couples by simply spending time with them. There are so many layers to a relationship that only the two people involved can feel the feeling and decide how they want to go about it.

At the end, if one does not feel the relationship is functional for her, then it's time to do something about it. As I learn, I feel more confident about my decision. I think of how unhappy I was, and how happy I am now. Even though my ex is still trying to annoy me in many ways, things are turning out to be all right. I feel like in our community, as soon as someone gets a divorce, everyone feels like they have a right to ask why. I remember many of my family members calling me, asking for explanations. They constantly asked, "What happened?"

In a way, people make one feel pressured into coming up with reasons. I don't quite understand why people think that they can mind other's business, and give themselves the right to do so.

My experience was that there were three groups of people. First, those who gave themselves the right to call me and give me advice without me asking them for their thoughts. I found them very ignorant and disrespectful, while at the same time, in my mind, I was wondering why they didn't practice what they preached, and why they didn't focus on their own problems. Many of them had many more problems than mine, but were in complete denial about them.

The second group was those who wanted to show me empathy, but acted as if getting a divorce meant the end of my life. They cried, and acted in a pitiful way toward me. This group offended me. My thinking was, "Don't feel sorry for me. Feel sorry for yourself, because you just don't get it."

The third group didn't know how to act, and pulled away for a while at the time when I needed them most. I had a lot of anger and confusion toward them, but as time went by I came to realize that everyone is different, and as long as they didn't hurt me by their actions, they were okay, and I let them be without judging them.

As time went by, I started to draw clear boundaries for myself, which is what I'm doing more of right now. I've learned more about assertiveness. I've learned that a person who doesn't know how to respect herself could not respect others, in the true sense. I'd appreciate it if you'd explain the three types of self-expression, and the balanced form.

Therapist: Well, that's a good question because, like anything else, if we lose that sense of balance, some form of our development will become arrested. By development, I mean mental and psychological. To refer this to assertiveness, there are three different types of behaviors that people use to be related to one another. We are social beings, meaning that we cannot live isolated from other humans. We need to connect and interact with others, and we need to learn to become productive for ourselves and our surroundings.

The three types of behaviors that people use to interact with others are aggressive, passive, and assertive.

Aggression is related to dominance, wanting to take advantage of others, and crossing other people's boundaries. Aggressiveness is when one expresses her or his rights at the expense, deprivation, or embarrassment of another. Aggression can become emotionally or physically forceful, not letting the other person express her or his rights.

Another one is passiveness, which is when one submits to others, and in the process lets herself become invaded and devalued by them. Passivity happens when a person submits to another's dominance behavior, putting her or his own wishes and desires aside to pay attention to fulfilling the wishes and desires of the dominant partner.

The balanced form is assertiveness, which is the ability for self-expression in healthy ways, without abusing the rights of others or crossing their boundaries. Some characteristics of an assertive person are that they are open, honest, can express themselves, are self confident, and give and get more respect.

Self-assertiveness means expressing one's thoughts and feelings in a way that clearly communicates the person's needs and intentions. It's a great way for a person to experience her or his true self.

We have to pay attention to the important fact that being assertive is different than being selfish. Acting in selfish ways means that one is violating the rights of others. These are destructive and aggressive acts instead of constructive and assertive ones. These two are the total opposite of each other. Until one learns the process, he or she is not able to differentiate between the two. Now, before we go any further on this, I have to remind you that the session is about to be over, and I would like to check in on how you are feeling.

After sharing some last minute feelings and going over the week's homework, we ended the session with some relaxation techniques, practicing them and focusing how to concentrate on each part of the feeling and to respond to it. Sara was given homework to monitor her behavior to see which category it belongs to; assertive, aggressive, or passive.

Session 8

The following session started with the same routine small talk and review of the past week's homework, which was challenging irrational patterns of thinking as they emerged. Sara was encouraged not to do things that made her feel uncomfortable to please others. Even though she'd made some changes, she still had some old habits that come back to her.

At this point, Sara started to cry, hard. It was a non-stop cry, and I just let her be. I offered her a glass of water and some tissues, and gave her some time to relax. This was a woman who was going through yet another grieving process. As I mentioned before, the grieving process happens when one senses a loss. There are stages one must pass through to be able to go through this process without being stuck in it. The first stage is denial. The second is anger. Then comes sadness, and then acceptance.

Sara was in a stage of anger, going toward sadness. Her anger was toward her parents for not guiding her though such an important decision, essentially forcing her to marry someone she did not love; anger toward them for not supporting her, now that she wants to get out and save herself and her children, and anger toward her ex-husband for manipulating her and her children.

As I explained previously, based on Sara's description of her husband, his method of control is passive-aggressive, meaning that he does it in a confrontational way, but non-directly. Spouses of these types of people, specifically at the level of Sara's maturity and awareness, can be damaged extensively. It will be a constant battle. Treatment of passive-aggressive people who are in complete denial of the stage they're in is very hard, and they usually do not seek treatment.

After giving Sara some time to herself, I started the process.

> **Therapist:** I can see that you feel intense pain when these memories are brought up. You probably experience a wide variety of feelings. It's good to pay attention to these feelings. They are all yours, and they are there for you to experience. Just be careful when it gets to be too engulfing.
>
> No feeling has the power to engulf you. It is *you* who has power over it, so be in control. A good way to do this is constant awareness of the state you're in, and the self-talk list we went through. Practice it routinely, and it will become a habit.
>
> Now, let me refer back to your question about why you were not taking any action. Why were you passive about it? You had responded to this, saying that as a part of your personality and your upbringing you were encouraged to be passive. You did the best you could, considering what your environment offered you. You can't blame yourself for doing what you knew was the right thing at the time. Your view of life was that you should do the best you could to make your marriage work. Now, you still have that same view, but have learned that in the process you have to feel satisfied about it, too. You've learned that if you feel dissatisfied, there's no point to the relationship. You have to take steps to let go of this

feeling of dissatisfaction. We cannot blame ourselves for mistakes, since they're a part of life. Besides, in your case, you weren't the one who picked your husband and your family. They were picked for you, and you were pushed into molding yourself into their expectations because of your beliefs. You cannot blame yourself for any of that.

Now that you're at another stage of your life, with a different point of view and perspective of life, you can make new choices with determination and hope. You accept the old choices because they were a part of your life, you think about them, learn from them, make sure you don't repeat the same mistake twice, and move on. This is called the acceptance of life as it throws itself at us. We do the best we can at each stage of life. With increased awareness and knowledge about ourselves, this gets clearer. What do you think?

Sara: Now, after your explanation, I see it the same way. It gets easier for me to look at it as a stage of life and a learning lesson, rather than as a time that was wasted. I think it makes the process of forgiveness easier.

Therapist: Many people have a misconception of forgiveness. Until we truly comprehend what it is, doing it and making it a part of us will be easier said than done. Forgiveness is a release of negative feelings toward someone. It is something we *feel*, not something we *do*. It's not a behavior or an action. It's something inward, a feeling. When we forgive a person, it has stages to it that we have to go through before we can truly forgive. Otherwise, it will be denial and escaping, not forgiving.

In addition, we know by now that denial is never positive for us. Forgiving is when we understand the situation, view it from the person's perspective, his or her level of maturity, both intellectual and mental, what brought him or her to the point of acting the way he or she did, and how we contributed to that action. Then we find ourselves feeling less resentment, anger, and hate toward the person, and more of a neutral feeling. We still might behave in ways to make sure the person does not damage us, or does not cross our boundaries, but we are in a state of light-colored inside toward the person. That is called true forgiveness; feeling neutral even if we have to go to self-defense mode. That way, instead of wasting our energy through anger and resentment, we are focusing on productive ways to find a solution for self-defense. It's when we let go of negative emotions toward a person, based on our level of awareness. Is it making sense?

Sara: You make everything make more sense, and become so comprehensible. I cannot tell you how happy I am to have come to you. I really do appreciate it. Now, looking at this, I do see many people who say that they have forgiven someone, but, when it comes down to it, you can see so much hate and anger still in them. It seems like it's something they say to make themselves believe it, but they don't really feel it or mean it. This is very dangerous. It's like they lie to themselves.

I try not to do that. I try to pay attention to how I really feel about a person who has hurt me, or who seems bad-intentioned. When I truly am willing to forgive, I feel free, I feel like I can walk toward liberation, I feel like I'm finally able to do what I wanted to do. I feel more like myself.

There's one area where I find myself struggling. What if my ex-husband's lifestyle affects my children negatively, and they're affected by it? That way, all my hard work to discipline them and to make sure they have a healthy environment will be wasted.

Therapist: From what I've heard and read from you, and what I see in you, you have a wonderful relationship with your children, and they seem to be learning from your side of the upbringing more that their dad's. It seems to me that your personality and your way of living are so strong that they're completely compensating for any shortcomings their dad might have. Sometimes when we are over-invested in a position, we cannot see it as clearly. An outsider's input will help with that.

Sara: You know, you're right. I know it most of the time, but sometimes I need reminders from sincere people to feel like someone is genuinely supporting me. At any time of my life, I've done the best I could, based on what I knew was the right thing. It might not seem as much of a right decision now, but I did it with a clear conscience at that time. When I decided to go ahead with the divorce process, I knew many of the obstacles that were in my way. I knew what I had to go through, not all of it, but much of it. Let me read you this.

I thought to myself, I will walk toward a city which has innocent children who have a flower of passion in their hands, a city full of peace, sincerity, honesty, passion, compassion, true love, true friendship, and no selfishness. Behind the sea is a city, and I had to build a boat. I knew I needed a lot of determination and hope to be able to go through it. I knew I had to experience a lot of rejection and disappointment, but I also knew that I was ready for it. I built the boat, got on it, and started to move toward the city. Little by little, I felt closer to it. It was an inward feeling that only I could experience; me and no one else, I could not explain it. It was my feeling, and belonged to me. I was ready to move toward the city of my passion, moving toward the city, passing thorough the waves, staying like a determined captain, holding onto the wheel, and not giving up until I got there, I was ready to go, even if that meant I had to go by myself. I will go forward, I will get away from this strange place, I will move away from this strange feeling of being untrue to myself.

Therapist: I enjoyed that. How much longer until you get to the city, and how does it feel, now that you're on your way?

Sara: I don't know how much longer, but it feels like I'm not lost, anymore. I'm very self-determined. I would love to hear your description of this, and how you see it.

Therapist: Well, there are different components to it. A self-determined person is one who makes responsible decisions based on reason and facts, rather than on impulsivity. In addition, she has a sense of making her own decisions rather than having the decisions being made for her.

Individuals get more satisfaction and benefit from activities that come from their intrinsic interest, rather than an extrinsic reward. When people feel like their lives are controlled by what others think and how they may be judged, and when they feel like they have to constantly shape their lives to please others, they get a sense of inferiority and mental blockage for what seems to be a lost sense of true self. Every one of us has a natural tendency to feel like we're in control of our own destiny, and this feeling gives us a sense of empowerment. However, because of the irrational thinking and irrational behaviors that have been imposed upon us during our upbringing, we may come to forget that we have the power to change our lives. We will absorb the role of letting others choose for us, tell us what to do, affect us too much, and control us, without knowing why or thinking whether that's right for us.

A person who has a responsible and determined attitude toward life has goals that are reasonable, according to her or his potential, limitations, and weaknesses, rather than what others think, and what is stereotypically more common. It means making your own decisions with a strong mind rather than a constantly changing one.

The self-determination process starts in childhood and persists throughout life. If one has not had a chance to learn it in childhood, then there is still a chance to practice it later on in life. Does it sink in?

Sara: It does. Like everything else, it's very personal. I mean, whether we consider ourselves self-determined or not depends on one's personality and life circumstances. 'I' is an internal feeling, not a set of behaviors.

Therapist: It's an internal feeling that comes from the person's behaviors, according to her or his life and personality. That is why it's naturally against every person aiming for self-growth to let others choose her life without considering what she wants. No one could know a person as she does herself. She is the one living with herself every second of every day, familiar with all aspects of her being, even the ones hidden from the five senses.

Only if one spends time learning about herself, does one discover so much she didn't even know existed. All of us have to try our ability to dig deeper into our state of being and discover the hidden aspects, the roots, and the source. There's so much to learn.

Sara: I can definitely feel this. I feel like I'm more self-determined than ever before. I feel like I still have a lot of work to do, but am so happy for the changes I've made. It was worth the fight.

Therapist: Time flew again. Let me review last week's homework with you, and go over next week's.

The session ended with a review of the last week's homework, reviewing Sara's memories, pattern of thinking, how she responded to situations, and getting a better picture of who she really is, what improvements she's made so far, and what other areas she wants to put more focus on.

Sara was encouraged to write her goals for the next day, weeks, month, six months, one year, two years, all the way up to twenty years. This was intended for her to think of a list of goals that matched her personality, her true passion, her strengths and weaknesses, and her priorities in life. Many of us go through life without having a hard look at this. She was encouraged to think about these goals and cross out the ones that didn't seem reasonable, or seemed like imitation rather than coming from her true sense of self. It was explained that the way in which she set goals strongly affects their effectiveness.

Then we reviewed steps toward setting goals, which included a positive statement of the goal, being precise about what it is, setting priorities, if there are multiple goals, writing the goals down, and starting with smaller goals and going to larger ones systematically.

Session 9

The following session, Sara came in ready to start, looking healthy and calm. As usual, we started the session after small talk.

Therapist: How was your week?

Sara: Good. I feel like a little girl who can't wait to come in and show you her homework. It's like a motivational factor. It's just eye-opening how thinking about these things, taking time to process them, and writing about them can change one's perspective on her life. The more I focus on my life and what I want to do, the more I see doors open up.

For example, I was writing my goals, how I want to be a writer, an artist, learn music, play tennis, but now my number one goal is to be a great mother and meld the other stuff into it. How I want to teach in a top university. While I was writing these down, and while I spent extensive time thinking about them, it came to my attention that some of these goals are not in concurrence with others when it comes to timing. Therefore, I had to make some adjustment to make them more reasonable. Now, this is the list I've come up with, but I need to work more on it. It's not done.

After taking time to look at her list, it came to my attention that she had too many goals and might need to think it through to make sure she's not pushing herself, and that she's being reasonable when it comes to achieving them. Sara seems to still have some of the irrational belief that she must be ideal; the same characteristics that she explained during the beginning of the therapy process. She's been able to change a great deal, but sometimes this part may come back without her being aware of it. I tried to help her become aware of this, and encouraged her to challenge her list of goals, based on that awareness. Being reasonable when setting goals is an important factor.

> **Therapist:** Let's discuss a number of general rules regarding goal-setting. One is that we focus more on the performance than on the outcome of goals, because in achieving goals there are some areas over which we have no control. There is nothing more disappointing than failing to achieve a personal goal for reasons beyond one's control. If we focus more on the performance or skills and knowledge that are being acquired during the pursuit of our goals, then we can keep control over them and draw satisfaction from them.
>
> Another very important factor is that when we focus too much on getting to a goal for the purpose of achieving something as a reward, whether the rewards are financial or emotional, for example, gaining recognition in the community. In the earlier stages, these factors will be motivating, but as time goes on and we achieve them, the reimbursement of achieving more at the same level

becomes less, and we find ourselves doing more to get the same level of satisfaction. This is where we lose that sense of balance, and may become obsessed with something. As time goes on, we find ourselves progressively less motivated by the same thing. In psychological language, we become desensitized to what motivated us at first.

For example, here in this column, when you say your goal is to organize educational classes and community work for your children, you have to focus on the steps, and what they're learning in the process. It means you're focusing on the performance, as you see them learn more and more by you organizing such environments for them. You get more satisfaction from it, and they're more nurtured by it. Another important factor in setting goals is having specific goals that are real, rather than idea or irrational, goals that are measurable, and that you can be confident and comfortable in achieving.

Sara: How do I know if my goals are reasonable or unreasonable?

Therapist: Goals may be set high in ways that are unreasonable, or unreachable at the time, because we let other people, like parents, media, society, or peers set those unrealistic goals for us. They do this in ignorance of our objectives, aspirations, and purpose. Another reason for this could be that we simply don't have enough information to form a clear understanding of what we're really trying to gain. If we set goals without having information and knowledge about them, we feel lost about what it is we really want in life and are looking for.

Sara: I think I do that, sometimes. I think, in some ways, I still may have the perfectionist in me. I've come to realize that being a perfectionist limits me in so many ways, not letting me get where I want to be in life, fully and with a sense of satisfaction, because in a changing world there is no perfection.

Therapist: That's true. The mistake many of us make is that we set our goals based on our best performance at all times. This will get us to some of the goals, but not others. We end up burning out. On the other hand, if we set goals that raise our average performance, then we can make it more consistent throughout our life.

If we set the goals too low, it could be due to the fear of failure, which results in not taking the risks needed for a more improved life. If one takes it too easy, one may set the goals unrealistically high as an excuse for him or herself to not get there.

Bottom line, if one is not ready to face challenges and fears, to risk some things in life, to stretch herself to move forward, one is likely to get stuck in one phase, never making any changes for the better, never unfolding and developing. Now that we've had a brief overview of goal-setting, think about this and see how you want to mold it into your own life. Okay, now I want you to think of the areas you want to work on as your goals. Let us categorize them into artistic, attitude, career, education, family, financial, physical, pleasure, and public service. Then we'll focus on emotional, mental, and spiritual growth. How do you see each one?

Sara: Okay, let me go in order.

Artistic, I do want to learn a form of music, which is my goal within the next year.

Attitude, I do think that I want to work some more on my irrational ways of thinking. I still have some anxiety. I still do want to please others. I still have some passive part to me, and I still do have some insecurities.

Even though I've improved, I still need to do more work. I want to feel truly liberated; liberated from any insecure attachments, liberated from any desires I can't control, liberated from any unwanted thoughts. I want to be able to live in total peace and harmony with myself. That's my main goal, I want to get to my fullest spirituality, I want to unfold myself and become self-actualized.

Regarding my career, I want to become a university professor. I love teaching, and with my degree and the knowledge and skills I have, I think I could do it.

Education, I think I'm where I want to be in regard to having a degree, but I do want to set a time every day for educating myself about something new. I specifically want to learn different sciences, like physics, biology, chemistry, and math, in an average level, in order to see how this world is functioning.

Family, I want to be the best parent I can be, I want to get respect from my extended family, and want them not to interfere with my life and tell me what to do. I wish I was closer to them, but have come to accept it as it is.

I also want to have a romantic relationship, and may even want to marry someone who can attract me on deeper levels. Financially, I want to have a comfortable life for me, my future, and my children. I don't want to waste my life being obsessed over having too much money or material things. I just want to have a comfortable life and a secure retirement, making sure that I'm not dependent on anyone.

Physical, I want to be healthy and take the steps necessary to achieve that. I like the way I look, and would not do any superficial thing to change it.

Pleasure, I want to enjoy my life, up to a point of not getting lost in finding that sense of pleasure. I want to look for pleasure as a quality, rather than quantity. This could be tricky if one is overly indulged in it. I want to see the world, take trips, read, write and help others. I find pleasure in these. Community work, I want to dedicate a large portion of my life to this. My ultimate goal is to discover my self and that inner peace the prophets experienced. I guess you call it self-actualization, and that's why I'm going through therapy; to help me get there.

Therapist: Now hold on to that thought, take it home, look over it with your list from last week, and compare the two. Make any changes you want. Put them in order, and hang them somewhere where you can see them, until you feel comfortable with them. Remember again, the goals have to be reasonable and reachable, and what your true self needs. Then write down what steps you're willing to take or are taking in order to achieve these goals. As you move forward with your life, unfolding your being and making new discoveries about yourself, you will learn to become less resistant to awareness. People need time and help to be able to open up to new information. However, many people become, in so many ways, comfortable or, for the lack of a better word become so used to living a certain way that may be the result of association with inhibitions, limitations, and self-controlling strictness. These blocks prevent these people from reaching a state of great freedom, vitality, true honesty to self, and as a result to others, wisdom, and a true sense of responsibility.

All these factors can be threatening to an individual who feels fearful of moving higher than his or her comfort zone. An explanation for this could be that the innate desire for freedom is a vulnerable state of being, which is associated with the inner-child complex. This caused some feelings of weakness, like vulnerability, shame, guilt, and rejection to come into play, and many people are not mentally strong enough or developed enough to be ready for the need to deal with these feelings.

Another important factor to consider would be that for people who have not had a chance to have a nurturing environment during their childhood, and may have experienced interpersonal trauma and abuse, either emotional or physical, many desires are, in a way, denied. If they want to start to become open to areas of experience related with such denied parts, it may involve some risk-taking, and that causes an overwhelming sense of anxiety that stops them from moving further.

The whole point here is that it takes time, encouragement, reassurance, and continuing effort to move to the process of individuation. During these therapy sessions, techniques like molding, support, sharing, and others are used to help you be drawn to the fullness of your personality, and to be desensitized to the associated fears of daring to desire and have needs and wants. Now, let me stop here and ask you how you're feeling and what you think about this.

Sara: My process of individuation did not start until

about two years ago. I didn't even know what it was. Now, looking back, I laugh at myself. The amazing part is that the denial stage you're talking about makes one blind to the state one is in. When I knew nothing about myself, I thought I knew a lot. Now that I know much more, I feel like there is so much I need to learn. When I decided to get a divorce, because it was just getting unbearable, I did experience the fear and anxiety you're talking about. The risk-taking was too much for me, even though I knew that it was exactly what I wanted. It was like what I explained to you, or you perhaps read in my diary, about my ex-husband's behavior during our separation. By the way, what did you think of that?

Therapist: There are many ways a partner tries to control his/her wife or husband. In your case, listening to you and reading sections of your diary and your homework, it seems like your ex-husband was controlling you by making you responsible for the separation. He was in complete denial of his role and, with his personality of wanting to look like the victim. He was probably enjoying the attention he was getting from some of the people surrounding him. He was putting the blame on you by saying things like, "Our marriage was perfect until …" It seems like your ex-husband went into a pattern of blaming you for his behaviors. He avoided accountability by blaming others, or you. For example, he said things like, "I did it because you…" or, "You just don't see what I do," or "Just show me how." It seems like another method he used was to control you by assigning status. This could be seen when he tried to put you down at what you do the best. He said things like, "Practice what you preach." Now, because your husband was the type who was subtly controlling, many of his behaviors were not visible on the surface, but were done passively and underneath, perhaps through manipulation. This could mean that it would take you longer to process it.

Another way your ex-husband seemed to have tried controlling you would have been his attempts to diminish you. By that I mean the belittling jokes you keep referring to in your diary, the laughing that seemed like making fun of something important to you, the offensive jokes, the mimicking, the ignoring, avoiding eye contact, turning away, the baffle gabbing, which means talking in ways intended to mislead or baffle you, making inappropriate sounds, and accusing you of being controlling, even though he wanted you to do the chores and be responsible for them, while at the same time he would call you controlling. Verbal abusers use these behaviors to gain a feeling of being in charge and powerful. This is seen whenever the abuser's suppressed fear and pain starts to come out. The abuser usually is scared of feeling the pain, and feeling any feeling, in general, and he projects this fear toward his partner, one way or the other.

Now, let's go back to you, Sara, because, after all, you're half of this picture. What I mean is that you chose to take this, and as a result, this lasted for as many years as it did. You could have made the changes sooner, but chose to wait. Now, let's look at that purely for learning, not blaming. It seems like in this marriage, and in every relationship you've had, for example with you dad, you were the caretaker, either physically or emotionally. This, by itself, is a controlling behavior. What people don't seem to realize is that just because we think something looks positive, that doesn't mean that it's in balance. We have to learn that if something is taking us away from our balanced state of living, then it's a bad thing for us. You took the role of a caretaker in your relationship, you wanted to look like the "ideal or nice girl," and did everything you thought your ex-husband wanted you to do, including making food every or most days, cleaning the house, doing groceries, doing most of the child care, and doing the laundry, even though you were going to school and sometimes working part time.

Somewhere, deep down within you, you believed that if you were nice enough, you could have control over everyone thinking you were an idea wife, which would then be feeding your picture of yourself as an ideal girl. What you didn't realize was that this niceness was really feeding your ex-husband's controlling behavior, giving him the right to raise his expectations even higher, and never questioning them.

You seem to have had a fear of rejection, as well. You were simply trying not to be rejected. At some points, you were trying to be controlling by criticizing your ex-husband. This relationship started the wrong way, with a series of lies and deceptions from you ex- and his family toward you. You knew from the beginning that you did not like what you saw, yet you tried to deny your feelings and suppress them. You tried to do more every time you felt like you were unhappy, causing you to resent him even more by thinking that you were doing all this and not getting anything in return. You could never connect with your ex-husband, because neither of you were ever authentically yourselves. It seems like he still is not, and may never be.

However, as we've clearly seen, you've come a long way and have made many changes, getting closer to being more authentic. Now you've learned how to take loving care of yourself, rather than attempting to control how others feel about you. You're also learning how to take the feeling of rejection. You're learning to take responsibility for your own feelings of wellbeing instead of being dependent on others to make you feel good.

In learning to take care of yourself, you would naturally stop pulling and pushing and being pulled and pushed by other's feelings, behaviors, and emotions. You're learning to speak your truth without blaming, judging, withdrawing, and criticizing. You're learning to stand up for yourself and set your limits, and make sure no one disrespects your limits. All this will help you overcome your fear and be liberated.

Now, let me tell you that the session is about to be over, and I want you to go over what I just said and write down your feelings related to it, what you saw as your contributing behaviors to the relationship, and what changes you've been able to make in yourself.

The session ended after Sara talked about how she felt, and a relaxation technique at the end.

Session 10

The following session started as usual with small talk and reviewing last week's homework. Sara seemed much more relaxed and stress-free. She seemed more focused, as well. I acknowledged this in her. Then I asked her about her week.

Sara: I enjoyed my week. I'm starting to learn to enjoy myself more and more. My sleep pattern is getting better and better. As soon as I go to bed, it takes me several minutes to fall sleep. I'm more relaxed and much more at peace with myself. I actually like my "me" times, now. I read, I learn about myself, I write, and I draw. It is a very peaceful feeling, a feeling I'm not able to get through anything else. Material things like shopping, partying, and the like, just don't give me that sense of satisfaction any more, I mean, I still do them, but much less than before.

During my week, I learned more about the feeling of love. I'm learning that a loving behavior is a personally accountable behavior that nurtures and supports each person's growth. It's supposed to make the parties involved feel supported, and feel compassion and understanding. I also learned that I put myself in controlling relationships because I learned that in my childhood. I learned that it was okay and normal for a woman to be controlled by a man, and that this was a sign of love.

Now, I see that controlling behavior is often unconscious, and its attempt is to get something like feeling safe, or love or attention. It can also be done to avoid something like being rejected, disapproved, or feeling lonely. A true loving behavior is one that is satisfying in and by itself, and no outcome is expected; one in which we do not expect anything back. Controlling behavior, on the other hand, is done with an expectation of an outcome attached to it.

In my case, I was controlling the situation because I wanted to look like the "perfect" girl, whatever that was. Now, I know what a false state I was in, because I was not being aware of myself. Now, I'm learning to love, in its fullest sense. I love my children, not because I want them to love me back (even though that would be great), or because I want them to take care of me when I get older, or because I want others to see me as a good parent. I do it because it just comes naturally. I'm learning more and more to do so. I guess that comes with my becoming more knowledgeable of myself and less needy of others. It's all about the intention, as you may say.

Therapist: That's right. It *is* all about intention, and not the behavior. One might do something that looks good, from an outsider's point of view, with a damaging intention, and one might do something that, on the surface, does not look good but with a productive intention. It's like the example of a knife mentioned by a seeker whose name I do not recall. Both a thief and a doctor use a knife to cut through a human's body, but the first one's intention is to rob another, but the second one's intention is to heal and save a life. They're both doing the same behavior, using the same tool, but the intention behind it makes a whole lot of different.

Most of us cannot see an intention behind a behavior, and as a result mislabel behaviors all the time. We label people as good or bad, based on a behavior we don't know much about. We can see a behavior, but we cannot see the thought and feelings that result in that behavior. In addition, sometimes the feelings we get try to give us a signal which, many times, we ignore.

The feeling one gets from a loving action with a pure and loving intention is very different from the one received with an intention of control or trading, even if the behaviors seem the same on the surface. For example, from your writings and your diary, it came to my attention that you felt that your father's intention, even when he was acting kind toward you, was to make you listen to him and go back to your marriage. That's why you did not receive the kindness positively. By then, you knew the intention behind it.

He didn't show you love because he was feeling compassionate toward you, or at least that's how you felt it. He showed you love to bring you back under his concept of the "ideal" girl who would not do anything to damage the family's "reputation," or to go against what your fathers wanted.

The intention I'm referring to can be anything and everything. For example, one can donate money or volunteer time to a worthy cause, purely for the pleasure one gets, or to get publicity, a tax break, or a place in heaven. Every one of these intentions gives the giver a very different feeling after the behavior.

Trying to control the outcome of a behavior is reflected in many situations. We see many so-called religious people who try to control the outcome of a behavior by trying to use [[[God as a limited concept. Defining God in a sense that will satisfy their basic need like a rewarding/ punishing God, a God that has preference, a God of imitation and fear not love etc.

When compassion has a higher place than controlling the situation, one learns to not judge things or humans, labeling them right or wrong. When parents give love to children in a conditional way, rather than as unconditional love, it seems to the children that they have to gain their parent's love by acting the way they approve of. It seems like they learn ways to try to get this love. Parents use anger, threats, sarcasm, punishment, criticism, judgments, withdrawal, physical or emotional abuse, money, shame, and other ways to control their children. Children should be rewarded for good behavior, but should not be labeled as a bad or good child because of the behavior. They should feel like they are loved no matter what, but that there are consequences to their behavior. Sometimes, this child, in the process of being good, may even deny his or her own feelings and take responsibility for other's feelings.

Children who are told that focusing on themselves is selfish may grow up wanting to continue the pattern of following other people's rules for their approval and attention. This means, for example, following the rules of a church, mosque, or any other religious center, without asking why she is following these rules or truly learning about herself in the process. This is an act of an imitator. Imitation usually does not get to the root of a matter, but deals with it on the surface. When you deal with something on the surface, the healing process is usually temporary, and has side effects. When you dig in and deal with an issue on the deeper layers, the healing process is a real one.

Other examples could be a person who is a community do-gooder, or people who sacrifice themselves, not because it's coming from their true passion, or as they may say from their true being or their hearts, but because it's coming from intentions and sources that are not pure in intention.

That may be a reason why so many people are confused by people who were labeled as some sort of a "wonderful" person, but then behaved differently. Too many times, we spend our time, or should I say waste it, judging people whose real identity we have no knowledge of. We may pass up a good opportunity to get close to someone or something, or may get close to someone or something we shouldn't, based on our judgments, most of which are not what they seem in the surface impressions. If we learn to increase our true knowledge and pass these primary steps, then we've opened a new door of deeper connections to the truth for ourselves. So, let's see how you see this. How can you related it to yourself?

Sara: I can see that I did not get unconditional love as a child. A lot was expected from me, especially because I was a girl. I mean I did feel like I was loved, but I also felt like I was neglected, somehow. I've always tried to get the approval of others, rather than being myself. I've learned to act in ways that would make them be pleased with me and love me. It seems to me that all the childhood training I got, trying to get the "love" from others, has led me to avoid my own personal needs, feelings, and behavior. I didn't show myself any compassion and love until recently. I thought it was selfish to do that. Now I know how ignorant I was.

Therapist: Can you identify your core feeling as a child?

Sara: A combination of feelings. However, the one that led to me wanting to get love would be shame. Somehow, I learned to feel shame if I didn't do what I was told, and what was expected from girls, stereotypically, in my family, which was that a girl was not supposed to be assertive, a girl would be a good housewife and nothing else, a girl would not share her husband's secrets with others, a girl would sacrifice herself for the marriage, etc. I went against that. I got educated, I got a divorce, and I started to learn to be assertive. At the beginning of each stage of change, I felt more shame than pride. Now, I'm starting to learn to feel pride rather than shame. I thought it was selfish to do that. Now, I know how ignorant I was.

Therapist: Shame is one of the most common forms of control. It's a false belief that we are essentially bad beings. People who as infants or children are neglected, shamed, or physically or sexually abused, have two choices about how to view these. They could see the truth that their parents were wounded themselves, and didn't know how to provide them with unconditional love, or that they could take the blame, and blame themselves for being a bad person who caused the abuse to happen, and that they were helpless to do anything about it.

The second category will learn to believe that the abuse or neglect was because they were flawed in some way, inadequate, unworthy, and unlovable. A core way of thinking, when shame overcomes us, is heard through our inner voice, "It's my fault they don't love me, I must be worthless, I'm not good enough, my bothers are better than me." This will lessen the power of despair, because if we're "not good enough," and that's the reason for others not loving us, then we still have a chance to be good to get love. This is denying the truth, and as long as we're in denial and ignorant about the truth, making changes is hard.

This pattern of thinking continues into adult life and we become addicted to feeling shame. Toxic shame is the form of shame that is false and pathological. Any emotion, up to a reasonable point, is needed for survival, but if it's not even-handed, it becomes dysfunctional; a blockage of growth rather than a tool for growth, and becomes toxic to the person experiencing it. Toxic shame is a result of childhood of abuse, rejection, exclusion, and neglect, depending on the severity of each one. For example, girls who have been given the message, during their childhood, that they are lower than boys, whether they've been told that directly or have experienced it by watching their mother, will grow up feeling an unreasonable amount of shame for even the most normal parts of life.

There are very few individuals who are able to resist authority without experiencing feelings of shame. Faith is a helpful element in this. Faith in the self, and in the world as an unlimited place with unlimited powers that can overcome any one authority or person, a world in which everyone has been given the right to feel his or her self, and to choose the way that soothes her/him. I want you to read this. Remember, a moderate form of guilt is okay to have, it's like a signal if we do something wrong, but shame is not healthy and has no use except blocking us.

Sara: Guilt says I've done something wrong; shame says there's something wrong with me. Guilt says, "I've made a mistake;" shame says, "I'm a mistake." Guilt says, What I did was not good;" shame says, "I'm no good." With guilt, the response is a desire for atonement, to make amends, to correct a mistake, or heal a hurt.

With shame, there are just painful feelings of depression, alienation, self-doubt, loneliness, isolation, paranoia, compulsive disorders, perfectionism, inferiority, inadequacy, failure, helplessness, hopelessness, narcissism. Shame is a sickness of the soul. It is the most poignant experience of the self, by the self, whether felt in humiliation or cowardice, or in a sense of failure to cope successfully with a challenge. Shame is a wound felt from the inside, dividing us from ourselves and from one another. I want to know more about this concept. I guess I'm more curious. What if someone has extreme feelings of shame? I know a number of people who have that.

Therapist: People who feel extreme shame may react with violence, drug abuse, low self-esteem, battering, harassment, blocking themselves from growth, no risk-taking, or many other forms of malfunctioning. Workaholics, compulsions, eating disorders, obsessions, extreme anxieties, depression, being pessimistic, etc., are some forms in which the individual either tries to block these feelings of shame or shuts down due to the intensity of these feelings.

A constant toxic feeling of shame may result from a feeling of falling short, and a weak self-image with no sense of power or control of one's life. People with this kind of emotion have an underlying thinking pattern that they are not good. Either sex can experience shame, but women seem to have it more frequently. Shame is a feeling of inadequacy, a sense of self-loathing, with very low self-esteem. To go back to the root of it, Eric Erikson, who created the stages of development, reported that humans go through each stage of mental growth at a particular time before they can start the next one. For example, during ages 3 to 6, which are the preschool years, children start to experience initiative vs. guilt. Preschoolers are very curious, and like to explore through imaginative play. A child who is not guided appropriately by his or her surroundings, especially parents, as to what is right and what is wrong may become confused in the process. If the adult's expectations are unreasonable, and they punish the child too severely for his or her mistakes, then he or she may develop a form of toxic guilt or shame. A child should be given the opportunity to make mistakes to be able to pass this developmental stage normally, without carrying excessive guilt, which may turn into shame in her later stages of life. As adults, we make ourselves believe that our best feelings come from others loving us and giving us what our parents did not. We continue planning our lives to get this. We must stop this pattern and learn that it is us and only us who must give ourselves the love we need to be able to share it with others and get love from them. Therefore, we have to start from ourselves and go further to others, not vice versa. We are, in a way, powerless over everything else except us. But, more and more, we see people who are trying to control everything except themselves.

Sara: The more I learn, the more my whole view of life changes. Things are making more sense. I think many people are living in ignorance, and it's unfortunate that the less they know the more they think they know.

I was one of them.

Just because they are educated, rich, or successful in one area of their life, they think they've mastered it all. They don't know that there is so much more to it. No wonder the level of stress-related sickness, mental health disorders, and relationship problems are increasing. No wonder we see people harming each other or the environment without feeling any negative emotion about it. It seems like we're moving backward. We're acting so childish and primitive. It scares me sometimes.

I don't see many people who are truly themselves, I constantly see people who are intensely affected by media, advertisements, what others think, and what's injected into them. These sources impose upon us what they want to make us believe. They, in a way, take advantage of our foolhardiness and lack of common sense; we don't even stop for one second to think, "Do I need that?"

They make us believe we need something so badly, and before we know it we have to have it, only to have no use for it. In one of the books I read, it talked about the concept of instant gratification, and how this primitive form may stay with us even during our adult life. I think most people have this. They see something and they want it, like an infant. They don't give it time to process and analyze it to see if they really want it, and somehow they don't stop this childish act until it gets worse, and it haunts them. What a vicious circle! How does a person who is not aware become aware of all of this?

Therapist: Well, there are many levels to awareness. We could go to many layers, and still unfold new ones. For the purpose of simplicity and the ability to comprehend, let's discuss the five levels of awareness that seem to be the major ones. People can function on several levels of consciousness at the same time. These could be an open expression, secrets, self-dishonesty, unconscious beliefs and feelings, and things that were not even considered.

On the first level, one expresses herself freely, clearly, and openly, depending on the situation; meaning that the subject of expression is comfortable for the person to talk about.

In the second one, which is the secret level, one is able to discuss some things and admit it to herself and to people she trusts, like her close friends or her psychotherapist. But what's important to note is that the person is aware of her thoughts and knows they're there; she just chooses to keep them within her for many different reasons, like not wanting to be judged, being careful, or not seeing it as necessary for others to know.

At the next level, which is the self-deception or self-dishonesty level, the person actively avoids, denies, or even opposes these thoughts within her by opposite thoughts. For example, a person who resents one of her parents starts to idealize that parent. Or, a person who has a negative emotion toward another person starts to tell herself the opposite.

Yet another example; a person who feels anxious toward something tells herself that it feels very comfortable.

Then comes the fourth level, in which the person does not admit to herself that these ideas even exist. That is called the unconscious level, meaning that they are there, but the person is not aware of them. This is because these thoughts and ideas are so uncomfortable to the person that they feel like they're conflicting with her sense of self. One attention-grabbing piece of information is that as people come to therapy or start to work on their self-discovery process, and as they trust themselves and their therapist more and become more self confident, they begin to shift these level four ideas into level three, and sometimes even level two. This is what is called by many the "insight."

The final level, or the level five of the awareness, contains those ideas that have not even been considered. In order to access this, one has to expand her knowledge, meet people with different beliefs and lifestyles, learn different patterns of thinking, expand her mind, and become more aware. As this goes on, they start to learn that there are other worlds outside the box, and that not everyone lives like their families and their cultures. At this level, the person becomes more tolerant and less bounded by a limited set of irrational beliefs.

Sara: So, where do you think I am right now? I mean which level of awareness?

Therapist: Well, a person can be at more than one level at the same time. It seems to me that you're certainly learning to access and acknowledge the denied thoughts. You're much more insightful than before, and are learning to access the deepest avoided parts of your unconscious. It also seems to me that you are learning to expand your views of life and are dedicated to increasing your knowledge of yourself and your surroundings. With this determination, you're walking through your path of self-discovery.

Sara: I see this, I evaluate it, and want everyone I love or care for to come and learn this. But it doesn't seem like they're into it, or they even care. Why is that? Why don't people just wake up?

Therapist: There is a certain resistance to awareness. People need time and help in becoming open to this awareness. When one gets used to living a certain way, which is associated with inhibitions, limitations, and being controlled severely, becoming a free and liberated individual with vitality, openness, wisdom, and responsibility becomes hard and threatening. It's like getting trapped in a comfort zone. Getting out requires effort and a certain risk they're not willing to take.

We humans get accustomed to our comfort zone, even if it doesn't do us any good. It takes courage and commitment for one to get out and move further. Our desires for freedom and a sense of innocence are innate, and are therefore associated with our inner-child complex. This makes it become vulnerable, because of feelings of weakness, shame, guilt, and rejection. As children, these emotions are hard to deal with, but as an adult, I mean someone who develops maturely, we learn that rejection can be dealt with by having a wider range of reactions. As a mature adult, we can learn that we can turn to different sources for support. Thus, self-affirmation becomes an easier task, but we know that many people are not ready for this much of challenge, and are scared to take further steps into becoming more unique individuals.

On the other hand, another explanation would be the fact that for people who have experienced some level of neglect, abuse, or even trauma, or those who have lived in an environment with many restricted expectations, having a sense of desire for oneself is a feeling that has been denied for so long. To ask such person to open this area and to experience such risks can be very anxiety-provoking for her or him. Therefore, such a person represses his or her potential to enjoy life and her or his new discoveries. As always, this path of self discovery takes time, determination, encouragement, reassurance, focus, and effort.

Now, I need to check on you and see how you feel.

Sara: I feel good, I just need some time to process the information and these different areas that I learned today.

Therapist: That's exactly what your homework for this week is. I have a little summary of it here, and then there are questions you need to answer to make you think about what you think, feel, and how you react, related to the levels we discussed. Before we finish, do you have any questions?

Sara: No, not right now. Except, do you want me to answer these questions every day, or just once during the whole week?

Therapist: There are six copies of the same questions for each day. You can pick a specific time that you read through this, think about it, maybe putting some pictures or other visual tool in front of you, doing some of the relaxation methods, and then thinking thoroughly about these questions.

Session 11

Next session started routinely with some small talk about the week's activities.

Sara: You know, during a couple of nights I felt this overwhelming sadness all over my body and soul. I don't know where it came from, but there seems to be a combination of factors. I'm just sad that even though I have a lot of people who love me, I don't have anyone I feel truly close to. I also feel like when I feel sad, I become creative. I brought a poem I wanted to share. Do you want me to read it to you?

Therapist: I would like that.

Sara: The road seems long,
My legs are tired,
The night is dark and I feel sad,

I don't know why, but something inside of me is calling me.

I listen.

There is this deep silence,

I listen some more, I hear nothing but silence.

How peculiar.

The silence has a message for me.

I go deep, deep into it, I close my thoughts,

The silence says,

"At the end of this seemingly long night, there is a dawn,

A daylight, a beginning."

It gives me hope, a true sense of hope.

Then it says,

"At the end of the seemingly long road, there is a purpose,

A purpose that is full of life and determination,

Keep looking at that purpose with ambitions,

Move forward, don't look back,

Keep yourself motivated and you will get there,

Stronger than ever,

Don't give up hope."

I thank that silence.

I move on with hope and determination.

Life is beautiful again.

Therapist: How do you feel after you write or read a poem like this?

Sara: Every time I write, I get a sense of emotional relief and spiritual connection. I feel lighter. It is somehow like therapy in its self-expression form. My father writes poems too. His poems are really good. I have been encouraging him to put them into a book. You know, I have many similarities to my father. But the limitations he experienced during his childhood and his environment just didn't let him grow to his full potential. He lost his sense of who he really was.

Therapist: What do you mean?

Sara: Well, my dad has this inner sense of being honest, not taking advantage of anyone, needing to be free and in peace. He had a lot of potential for what we call spirituality, or connection to the bigger picture, but throughout his upbringing, being the oldest child of a very traditional family. There were always very high expectations of him which were extremely unreasonable. Most, all, his brothers and sisters had expectations from him.

He worked really hard to get really high, in a business sense, in his life; but nobody was ever proud of him. On the other hand, the higher he got up the ladder of success, the higher the expectations. I don't know of anyone in my family who's given my dad unconditional love. They have a habit of gossiping about each other. I don't know how you can gossip about your own family.

My dad believed that you keep the family's problems within family. I took that from him, as well. For example, no matter how much trouble he had with my mother, when it came to outsiders, he always acted as if things were great between the two of them. I have never seen my dad complaining about life. But I always knew he had a lot of unspoken words, I knew he had a lot of pain inside that he had denied for so long, and that at one point in his life he used opiates to forget them. Now, he is, in a way, addicted to this opiate, even though he doesn't admit to it. One of my biggest hopes is to help him overcome this addiction. I don't think he'll listen to me, though. He's too deep into the denial phase. My father rewarded other people's expectations by giving them more. I don't know why, but he rewarded the aggressor. He would never defend himself, and instead would just withdraw and give them more, just to shut them up. I remember that my dad was honest in his business. He was careful to take care of his employees and to not to take advantage of anyone. But he was extensively damaged, because of his very rigid traditional beliefs and his role-taking behavior.

As I said before, my dad and my mom were not really happily married. Their relationship is getting a little calmer, since they're getting older, but they never had a loving, peaceful marriage. In this process, our upbringing, as the family's children, had a lot of obstacles. We had a lot of good times, as well as the bad times. Since a while ago, I feel less and less of an anger and more and more of a double image of what was going on. I do remember love, family gatherings, vacations, support, parties, a nice life with servants, and sometimes even chauffeurs, being the center of all the family, and other fun things. So my childhood life, I think like many others, was a combination of everything. I would like to read this poem for you, which I think is relevant.

Therapist: Sure, go ahead.

Sara: My heart full of love,

I was born with it,

I came to this world with the intention of giving love,

Receiving love, and finding myself.

Somehow, in the process,

I lost that very basic need.

Then I found myself looking for it, trying hard to reach it.

The harder I tried, the more unreachable it got

I was so occupied with chasing it

That I didn't have time to stop myself and think,

What am I doing?

What is it I am looking for?

What am I chasing?

Where is this chase taking me?

I am chasing something I was born with,

It is already in me, I just have to find it

By looking deep into myself

And showing that I care.

It is time to change,

It is time to wake up,

To wake up from this endless illusion to that unlimited reality.

I am ready.

I am ready.

Therapist: It's wonderful that you've found a healthy way to express yourself. Self-expression is one of the most healing processes. What you called unspoken words when you were talking about your dad, that's a reality many individuals face. They don't learn how to express themselves, live their lives in denial, suffer many mental and psychological blockages, and never feel liberated.

Unspoken words become like cancerous cells. They start building up, and if not healed will destroy the affected area, and ultimately the whole person. I think this is a good time to talk about defense mechanisms. Then I need you to take the information with you and do the homework. What do you think about that?

Sara: That's a good idea.

Therapist: Okay then. Psychological defense mechanisms are an important aspect of a person's mental growth that he or she must become familiar with. These are psychological strategies that individuals use to cope with the reality of life, and to maintain their self-image in one piece.

All of us use many different defenses during our lifetimes but these become pathological if they're used all the time, and lead to maladaptive behaviors that threaten the person's wellbeing. We have pathological, immature, neurotic, and mature types of defenses.

Pathological defenses are the those that prevent the person from being able to deal with a real threat and see reality clearly. An example of this would be a person who is so deeply in denial that there is a problem; a controlling husband who says his marriage is "perfect," an alcoholic who says he is not addicted to alcohol, a person who keeps on making the same mistakes over and over again, destroying her or his life, and keeps on blaming everyone but herself for the mistakes, etc. An immature type of defense is the one used in childhood and adolescence, but mostly discarded in adulthood, since they may lead to socially unacceptable behavior. As children and teenagers we can't see reality as it really is. We see the surface part of everything, people, places etc. But as we grow, our ability to comprehend should be growing, if we're being nurtured in a healthy environment.

The other type of defense, which is neurotic, is the one that does not deal with reality and can cause many problems in all areas of life, especially in interrelationships and enjoying life.

The last defense, which is the mature defense, is used by "mentally healthy" adults.

Let's put them into levels according to severity of problems they may cause in the person. Then try to process it and reflect it back to yourself.

Level 1 defenses are the ones that are almost always pathological, because the person uses them to rearrange external reality so he or she won't have to deal with it. These are denial, distortion, and delusional projection. An example of denial is a person who refuses to accept reality. We see people who deny they have a problem, despite the obvious signs of having one.

The next one is distortion, which is when someone reshapes external reality to meet internal needs. This would be a wife who is extremely unhappy in her marriage, but will reshape her reality of what she sees in a way to be able to get some form of inner satisfaction.

In the next defense, delusional projection, one projects his or her inner blockages onto that of the other. This is a person who suffers from extreme anger and sees everyone else threatening her in an angry way. This is called delusional, because it is, in its extreme forms. Before we go any further with this, I want to ask what you think of this.

Sara: I can't tell you how many people I know in my family and among my friends who are in absolute denial. They use that form of defense to escape from reality. I used that sometimes, myself. I was in denial that I was in an unhappy and distressful marriage. I was in denial that no one in my family truly valued me for who I really was, I just received fake compliments, but they didn't truly know me. I was in denial that I had to make some changes to make my life fuller. It wasn't until recently, within the past few years, that I've become more aware and have started working on this. I was in denial that my dad used opiates, I was in denial that my mom and dad's marriage had a lot of obstacles that damaged us, and it wasn't until I was able to finally get out of that denial that I started working on them.

Therapist: And always remember that just because one denies the reality does not mean that it is not living with her. It's still there, but if one doesn't accept it, it will have control over the person rather than the person having control over it. So, your childhood shortcomings were there in your unconscious, whether you denied them or not. But, by denying them, they had control over you, causing blockages in your inner growth. But when you acknowledged that they exist, accepted them, and moved forward with your life; you gained control over the feelings that come to you. You process the feelings, and your feelings work with you, not against you. You have control over these not-so-pleasant memories, rather than them being in control. It's not about whether something unpleasant and dark exists or not. Life is a combination of dark and light, pleasant and unpleasant. What matters is whether we have the ability to be in control of the dark when we face it.

Sara: That's true. The more I become honest with myself and see my life as it really is, rather than wanting to believe that it was and is "ideal," the more I'm able to take it where I want to take it, rather than being lost in a false world. I think today I'm in my poem-reading mood. Can I read you one more?

Therapist: Sure, go ahead. I do enjoy your poems a lot, and I feel like they, by themselves, are therapeutic for you. They're a way of expression, both those you write yourself or the ones you use from other poets.

Sara: That's correct. I don't usually feel bored or lonely, because whenever I am by myself, this writing gives me a sense of inner satisfaction. Here's the poem.

I said: I need you.

He said: I am here.

I said: I don't see you.

He said: I am within you, think of me and I am there.

I said: but my thought limits you, you are more than that.

He said: free your thought of the limitation

I said: the walls are too hard to tear down.

He said: not with your power

I said: I feel powerless.

He said: that's your mind's eye,

Don't look with your mind's eye, look with your heart's eye.

I said: what is my heart's eye?

He said: experience it.

I said: how?

He said: want it.

I said: how?

He said: choose it.

I said: I feel so lost and confused.

He said: look within you, clear the dust, throw away the garbage,

Take all the useless belongings off your shoulder, then you'll feel light.

The lighter you feel, the clearer your vision will become,

When you get a clear vision, pick your path.

Don't imitate, don't pick out of fear, don't pick to please others,

Pick with love and determination.

Then you'll know.

I said: Then I'll know what?

He said: Then you'll know the answer to your own questions.

You don't need me to tell you, because everything I have, you have, as well.

You just have to dig in and do the work.

Everyone can get there.

Basically, this poem came the other night, when I was meditating. I was so overwhelmed by a couple of unfair treatments I got through my divorce and how things, sometimes, are not what they pretend to be and how there was nothing I could do about it. I was thinking about what people will do for money, how greedy they can get, and how they can literally destroy families without even being conscious about it.

I didn't know how to react and what to make of it when I meditated, and this poem came to me. Writing these poems make me feel good. When I think of my life, I want to have a peaceful life, and I think that is the ultimate definition of happiness. I don't need much. I just want to focus on my writing to transfer what I know to others. And I want to focus on myself. The rest would be extra. These are my main passions. I don't know why I jumped so much off the topic, but I'm ready to listen more to the defenses, because I want to see which ones I'm stuck with.

Therapist: I really liked the poem. I need to ask you this first, and then I will go to the defenses. When is your peak time of writing these poems?

Sara: It really depends. Sometimes when I wake up early in the morning to meditate. Sometimes when I'm praying or connecting to nature. Sometimes when I feel an emotional pain. And, sometimes, when I feel this inner joy, love, and satisfaction for life. I get this a lot, the more I organize my life, and the more I let go of the extra baggage, as you say, the less pressure I feel. I've found myself more and more in peace and able to let go of what I need to let go of. On the other hand, I feel like I have fewer attachments. There is so much beauty in life that I just wasn't able to see, because I was constantly fixing my ex-husband's damage. I always knew that I had so much potential. I was always viewed by others as someone special. If I picked a friend, they would consider me their best friend. I knew how to get love and show love, but now I'm learning to do all these, but at the same time be true to myself rather than wanting to please others and ignore myself.

The more I learn to do this, the more naturally it comes, and I don't even have to try anymore. I've found myself more and more wanting to have a private life. I want to read, focus on my children's future, get mentally and spiritually advanced, write, exercise, and go around the world. I want to surround myself with a few good-hearted friends, rather than many "friends on the surface," if you know what I mean. These are my goals.

I dream of being an element in my dad dealing with his addiction. I'm not setting my hopes high on this, but it's something I will think about. I want to keep a clear boundary between me and my family. Their point of view is different than mine, and I want to make sure they're not allowed by me, again, to tell me what to do. If they're willing to respect that and value me the way I am, then I would continue my relationship with them, in a balanced form. If they can't respect me that much, then I guess I have to separate and go my way. I don't know why I, all of a sudden, started to talk about this but the fact that in your sessions I can freely talk about anything that comes up makes me feel so good. I don't get many chances to do that, with my personality. I'm usually listening to others rather than talking about my personal problems. Okay, I let it out for now, and am ready for you to talk about defenses.

Therapist: The whole point of therapy is to go with the person's needs. In order for the healing process to be happening, the person has to become the center of it and be completely engaged in it. Humans are complex creatures, and can't be treated as a simple machine. There are many levels to a human, only some of which we've been able to explain. But the interesting thing about it is that when one learns the mechanism of a human's functionality in one part, she can reflect it to her other parts as well. For example, in many senses, a human's mind is a reflection of his/her body.

Sara: What do you mean? Can you give me examples?

Therapist: For example, the body's immune system and how it functions; how its cells let in friendly cells, and they defend themselves against the enemy, how they fight disease-causing bacteria. When one pays attention, one can't help but notice that the immune system's function is similar to the concept of assertiveness in human psychology.

We say that a balanced human being attracts what is beneficial and resists what is harmful to him, or at least should learn to do so. Assertiveness is a balanced form between aggressiveness and passiveness. An aggressive person may drive away many constructive elements and a passive person may be a magnet for many harmful ones. But someone who learns to be assertive becomes skilled at knowing what to drive toward and what to drive away. I won't explain assertiveness too much, since we talked about it in detail during the previous sessions. But this example was used for clarifying the subject. How is it making sense?

Sara: It's making perfect sense.

Therapist: The session is about to be over. We'll continue with the discussion of defense mechanisms and relating them to your personality during the next session. Now, let me ask you how you feel.

Sara: Full of hope and looking forward to life.

Therapist: That sure is a great feeling to have! Problems are part of life, but how we decide to face them is the main factor of how we feel.

The session was over and Sara was given homework to practice what was discussed during the session.

Sara is making great progress, because she is extremely engaged in her healing process and is aware of what's going on. She wants to make changes, and is very committed to it. She has many skills that are contributing factors to her progress, as well. Not everyone who comes to therapy is that motivated. Many want quick fixes, not root-oriented changes. Many others come in just to see therapy as an adventure, and yet, a large number come in who are not really seeking any changes.

Session 12

The following session started with small talk, as usual, and asking about Sara's previous week.

Sara: I want to start the session with one of my poems.

Therapist: Sure, that's always a pleasure.

Sara: This came to me when I was in one of my silence moods. Sometimes, the way I meditate is that I go into this focus mode, and I imagine me as a small part of the universe, and then at the same time the universe as a small part of me. Then I go to a complete silence mode. After that, I do some prayer, and then I write my poems. Here it is:

You can go to your church,

Your mosque,

And your pleading place,

To pray,

But my praying place is right here,

In my heart with my beloved.

You can go to the distance to find serenity,

but my quiet place is right here,

In my heart with my beloved.

You can go through many obstacles to feel a bliss,

But my blissful feelings is right here,

In my heart with my beloved.

You may do so many things to feel what I feel,

All I do is feel the silence inside me,

To reconnect to the one I was supposed to be,

The one I was born to become.

I am me, and you and me can become one

Only if you find your silent place, too.

Let's walk together, hand in hand, with love and in harmony."

After a deep breath and having a quiet moment, Sara continued.

Sara: This week I thought a lot about the defense mechanism you talked about. I thought about how much denial I was in, and how I didn't even know that this was one of the most basic defenses. I thought about how many people I know who are stuck in there, and will probably always stay there. I feel myself being attracted to this self-discovery process. I can't stop it, and the more I get into it, the more I feel alive; alive in its real sense, not in a superficial way. I want to listen to you explain the rest of defenses, and want to see which ones I'm caught in.

Therapist: I like your poems, every one you've shared with me. They are so meaningful and touching. Now, you mentioned defenses. Defenses are very important aspects of a human psych. One needs to learn them to see where one is, in order to make steps forward. We went over the first level of defense, which included denial and delusional projection. In your example, when I was reviewing your homework, it seems like a good representative of this would be when your ex-husband blamed you for wanting to get a divorce. The way he twisted the story in his mind is a good illustration of a delusional projection. He made up stories (or twisted a factual story) to go with what he wanted to believe, and to project it on others rather than you or himself. Some of your ex-husband's stories about why you wanted to get a divorce were examples of delusional projections. His stories were not making sense, and it didn't take a scholar to figure that out.

Your divorce, standing up for yourself, and making these changes, were so "out of character" for you that he couldn't believe it, so he started to believe his own delusional story.

Then I read through your diary. You said, "Finally, I came to realize that this road I have to go by myself. It was a wavy ocean, but I had already gotten on the boat and had the wheel in my hand. The waves scared me, but I focused on the other side, where there was a beautiful island waiting for me. There were dangers on the way, there were risks, but I was determined to go through it, I was lonelier than ever, but I felt like I had something super-powerful backing me up, what it was, I don't know, but for me it was real, and don't you dare tell me it wasn't." How are you feeling?

Sara: That's as close as it can get. People pretend so much. They live as if they're on stage, acting. I'm just tired of those who act. I see religious people acting as if they're religious, all to get money, power, or attention. I see all sorts of people doing all sorts of things just to impress others, or to have their own needs met. I'm interested in people who are real, and true to themselves and to others. Those who don't act, but just are. There aren't that many of them. I'm sorry, I keep going on and on, and I really want to hear about the defenses, besides the first category, which was denial and delusional projection.

Therapist: That's okay. I'll talk about it now. We talked about the first defense. Now, the second group of defense mechanisms includes fantasy, projection, hypochondria, and passive-aggressive behaviors. This group of defenses is used by many adults and adolescents. If one just uses them every once in a while, these may adjust distress and anxiety imposed by other people or the real world. For those who use these on a regular basis, they're considered to be immature defenses, and lead to serious problems in the person's ability to cope with the real world.

In fantasy, people draw back into fantasy to resolve inner and outer conflicts. For example, these people would go into a made-up and imaginary world to escape their problems, rather than concentrating on a solution. In projection, the person blames another for his feelings. Prejudice and severe jealousy may come from this type of defense. In the passive-aggressive type of defense, which was what we assumed your ex-husband used a lot, the person expresses his aggression toward another indirectly.

In the last defense, which is acting-out behavior, the person directly expresses an unconscious wish or impulse to avoid being conscious of the emotion that goes with that impulse. For example, a person who is very angry and acts out in an angry way may have some very painful emotions that he's trying to hide, because he's not ready to face them.

Then comes level three of the defense mechanisms. These are fairly common in adults, and many normally functioning adults use them. These may have short-term benefits, but long-term problems in relationships and daily life, and enjoying life in general. These are intellectualization, repression, reaction formation, displacement, and distortion.

Intellectualization is when one tries to separate oneself from emotions, thinking, not acting.

Repression is when the emotion is conscious but the idea that is behind it is absent. For example, "I'm feeling really sad, but I won't think about it."

Reaction formation is to act completely opposite from what one wants or feels, for example taking care of someone when you want to be taken care of. This will or may work in short run, but will break down in the long run.

The other defense at this level is displacement, which is separating an emotion and redirecting the intense emotion toward someone or something that is less unpleasant or threatening in order to avoid dealing with what is frightening or directly threatening.

Another defense is dissociation, which is a temporary

and extreme adjustment of one's personal identity or temperament to avoid emotional suffering.

Then there is the last level of defenses, which are common among the most mentally healthy adults. At this level, the individual can use these defenses to master his pleasure and feelings, and to integrate many of the conflicting emotions and thoughts and still make them be effective. These are sublimation, altruism, suppression, anticipation, and humor.

Sublimation is converting negative emotions into positive actions. This is an example of someone who turns his anger toward someone and does some kind things for another person.

Altruism is when one gives constructive services to others that brings himself a sense of satisfaction.

Suppression is the conscious decision to postpone paying attention to an emotion or need in order to cope with the present reality, but then the emotion is attended to and processed.

At a later time, anticipation is a realistic planning for future unpleasant events.

And humor is an over-expression of ideas and feelings that gives pleasure to others.

Now, I know that was a lot of information, I need you to look at this and let me know if you're ready to reflect these to you and your surroundings. Let's use this example; how would you cope with a painful event in your life? As we all know, experiencing painful and unpleasant events is a part of life, and something no one can escape. How one copes with it makes the whole difference of what effects it has on the person.

Sara: I had some of the level one, which were denial, which I talked about. But within the past few months, and more now than even, I find myself using more of what you call altruism. I develop and express compassion for others who are suffering as I have suffered. For example, I started having a website with information, having seminars, and writing books. I also do some form of sublimation. I redirect my emotionality into socially and culturally constructive and desirable activities. I do the same with my children. I involve them with my projects, to make sure they get a sense of this. How about humor? I see people who seem emotionally/mentally immature, but use humor a lot. Does that mean that they're using a level four defense?

Therapist: You have to pay attention to be sure that the hostile humor is a level two defense mechanism, and does not go with this category of more mature defenses. This is more of a wit humor.

Sara: Oh, okay. Another one that I use is finding a positive or underlying meaning or purpose in the suffering I go through. This has helped me bring good out of it, or discover something productive from it. For example, as a result of this divorce process I went through, I truly came to realize that I had to work on my mental, physical, and spiritual being, and that it was me, and only me, that truly cared about me. And if I didn't pay attention to these realizations, that I would not be able to help anyone else, in the true sense. I also learned to be more organized, more independent, and more self-sufficient, and many other positive characteristics that this process helped me get to. When it comes to the level three defenses, I guess I used to use a lot of repression, and still use some of that. For example, I pushed many of my memories into my unconscious. I pushed away many of my unpleasant memories during my marriage and childhood because I wasn't ready to deal with them.

When it comes to intellectualization, I don't think I did much of that. I've started to use a lot of reasoning in the way I function, but I still feel my feelings, actually much more now than before. Even though, for a little while, when I was going through the divorce process, I started to study and write extensively about the theory behind emotional abuse and passive-aggressiveness, which I thought was what my ex-husband was suffering from. Maybe that was intellectualization in a way, because I couldn't handle the feelings at that time.

There is also the fantasy defense. I guess I did some of that too. I imagined myself writing about all my experiences, my books helping a lot of people, and me using that money to build educational centers for children who can't go to school. That fantasy took me to a good place, but I knew it was a fantasy. It saved me for the time I held onto it. Now, if I want to see which level two defensive mechanisms I use, or used to use. I have to say it used to be some form of projection, but not in a delusional level which was, I guess, a level one defense. I used to attribute something that was true for me at an unconscious level to someone else. So one question is, when is it that a defense mechanism becomes adaptive, and when is it pathological, because you said all these defenses can be used by adults to adapt to life.

Therapist: Remember that what we call a mental illness is, in reality, a manifestation of a person's pathological adaptive response to events in his life. When a defense is used rigidly and inflexibly, is based on past needs rather than present problems, leads to significant problems in relationships and functioning, leads to distortion of emotions, rather than enhancing them, then it is considered to be pathological.

Looking at you, you used to use a lot of denial, and as a result that caused problems, including anxiety, in you. Now, you're learning to use a more mature level of defenses as you move forward in the process of self-discovery, as you do that, dealing with life's obstacles becomes more possible for you.

Sara: Life is truly like a passage. All my life, I tried hard to get educated, to have a nice house, to have a nice car, and to have wonderful children, but after I had all that, I was still feeling lost. Actually, more lost than ever, because now I didn't know what else to go after. I was not much of a so-called materialistic person. When I saw all these women looking for designer clothes and spending all their money on their looks, I felt it was funny. I mean I did and still do care about how I look, dressing nicely, and looking well groomed, but it's not like an obsession for me; it's just something I do to look well-groomed and taken care of. This passage that we call life has one true meaning to me, and that is to know who I really am. To find my true self, and I believe that the rest will come along. I see many doctors and rich people who are truly not happy, or not in peace with themselves. Actually, many of them are overly stressed, so what is their education or their money really doing for them?

Sometimes, it makes them more omitted from the meaning of life. They get so focused on that one area of life that they totally forget the whole picture. I was kind of like that too, but deep down inside I knew I was looking for something full of meaning. I see people who go through a lifetime without making a change, without really growing. Only their physical body grows, but nothing else. What a waste!

I wrote this poem when I was thinking about a friend of mine who is a successful doctor, and considers himself religious, but is very limited in his way of thinking. He has very traditional ways of thinking that seem to be blocking him from growing as far as he can grow. But at the same time, this friend is so arrogant and narcissistic that he doesn't see anything beyond what he believes in. His way of thinking is something like this, "I do good, so God will give me good in heaven," like a trading system with a limited God that he made up in his mind.

I see a lot of people like him, or I see those who totally and single-handedly reject the notion of God altogether, as if God is something outside of them. They look at the limited aspects of what they've been taught, and since it doesn't appeal to them, rather than searching for what it really is, they deny it altogether. How can you deny something so obvious? You can't deny something that is everywhere. I believe in the multifaceted being, and have my reasons. I also do a lot of scientific studying to learn more and more, because I believe that all life and its different levels and forms are really a reflection of one anther. My whole life, I've been looking for this meaning. I choose my degrees based on that. I chose physiology to learn how the human body works, and then choose psychology to learn how the human mind works. I've also read and investigated spiritual books about Zen, Buddhism, Tae, Kabala, Islam, Sufi, Angha, and a wide variety of others.

I've applied these techniques on myself, and myself only, made a lot of changes, and am in the process of making more and more changes. I think life is change. It keeps moving forward, as one's body grows, so should one's mind and core being. If one gets trapped in a phase, then one is making herself predestined to waste, and is blocked from experiencing a full life.

Many times, changes are not what the outside people might expect. For example, Buddha left his family behind to go and feel his sense of being, and Mohammad went to Hara a few years before he was ready to lead his people. I'm sure all these folks were greatly judged by the people of their time, but at that point of their being they were not concerned about others judging them. All they cared about was to find what they had seen a glimpse of, to really feel and experience it. Here is the poem I wanted to share with you:

"Raise your head, be my moon,

Make me wonder, make me fall in love,

Make me proud,

Be my shinning light in the dark of this wavy ocean.

Give me your beautiful eyes,

Let me stare at them,

Let me drain into them.

I am still going strong after all this suffering,

Come and numb me to the pain,

Come and make it painless for me.

The moon seems to be ashamed when your beauty reveals itself,

The ocean seems to be calmer when it feels your presence,

My heart pounds faster and heavier when you're close.

Give me your love, let me be,

Let me feel, let me have.

And even if you don't, I will still accept it,

With all my heart, with all my essence."

Therapist: Thank you for sharing that with me.

Sara: You know what, Doctor? I've started thinking more deeply about life. It seems like in my process of self-discovery, I have become more compassionate and aware towards what is happening around me, and how it is affecting everything else. I was reading something the other day that made me start writing this part, which I would like to share with you. Some of these points were made by the person whose name, unfortunately, I do not remember. I totally agree with his points and started writing about it.

Here it is:

When I look at the world and its history, I can't help noticing that the two most powerful psychological forces in human history seem to have been violence and greed. The degree of slaughters that have been committed throughout history all over the world—many of them in the name of God or religion—is truly preposterous. Some examples would be that of Christians sacrificed in Roman arenas to provide a highly sought-after spectacle for the masses; or victims of the medieval Inquisition, who were tortured, killed, and burned in the *autos-da-fé*; the mass slaughters on the sacrificial altars of the Aztecs; and the many more examples that would take hours to describe and mention.

The very tool that's supposed to be helping us become more in harmony with our world, I mean religion, has become a tool for destruction. However, the difference between the past and today is that, in the past, violence and greed had tragic effects for the people involved, but did not threaten the whole picture. It also did not seem to impose a danger to the ecosystem as much as it does now. It seemed like nature was able to recycle and recover within a few decades after the violence. But now, in the twentieth century, with technology and the pace it's moving forward, industrial production, population increases, atomic energy, etc., seem to have a different effect, one that is not temporary and one that is going to be hard if not impossible for nature to recover from. This past century has been the fastest one, when it comes to technological advances.

We've made more progress in a single year than an earlier period's entire century. Unfortunately, this intellectual progress wasn't matched with emotional and moral growth, which only comes true a true sense of self-actualization. We are, in a way, exterminating ourselves with our technological advancement. There are more mental health problems than ever, there's more violence, more relationship problems, more people who want to take advantage of others, and no one seems to be taking this seriously. We've learned about nuclear energy, we've sent out spaceships, we've been able to transmit sound and color all over, we've cracked the DNA code, and have started genetic engineering.

But our emotional being has not made any advancement, and is actually very primitive. We're pretty close to where our ancestors were at the Stone Age. I read this sitting in an office waiting, and wrote it down. I wish I remembered the writer. Besides what I wrote above, he wrote something else which I copied into my notebook because it seemed really truthful to me.

He said, "Among these are industrial pollution of soil, water, and air; the threat of nuclear waste and accidents; destruction of the ozone layer; the greenhouse effect; possible loss of planetary oxygen through reckless deforestation and poisoning of the ocean plankton; and the dangers of toxic additives in our food and drinks. To this we can add a number of developments that are of less apocalyptic nature, but are equally disturbing, such as species extinction proceeding at an astronomical rate, homelessness and starvation of a significant percentage of the world's population, deterioration of the family and a crisis of parenthood, disappearance of spiritual values, absence of hope and positive perspective, loss of meaningful connection with Nature, and general alienation. As a result of all the above factors, humanity now lives in chronic anguish, on the verge of a nuclear and ecological catastrophe, while in possession of fabulous technology approaching the world of science fiction. Modern science has developed effective means that could solve most of the urgent problems in today's world—combat the majority of diseases, eliminate hunger and poverty, reduce the amount of industrial waste, and replace destructive fossil fuels with renewable sources of clean energy. The problems that stand in the way are not of an economic or technological nature. Their deepest sources lie inside the human personality. Because of our human failings, unimaginable resources have been wasted in the absurdity of the arms race, in power struggles, and in pursuit of "unlimited growth." These failings also prevent a more appropriate distribution of wealth among individuals and nations, as well as a reorientation from purely economic and political concerns to ecological priorities that are critical for the survival of life on this planet."

Then he went on discussing that there needs to be a

system of human transformation into individuals who are capable of peaceful coexistence with each other. At the time, to some, it may seem undoable. But modern psychology, like transpersonal psychology, which is trying to integrate spirituality with the new paradigm of Western psychology, seems to be offering some useful strategies to do that. There were five areas that he focused on, and I wrote them down.

These were: Development of a new image of the universe, and of a more comprehensive understanding of human nature, and of the psyche replacing or adding to the behaviorist and Freudian models, new understanding of the roots of malignant aggression and human violence, new insights into the nature of insatiable greed, experiential approaches facilitating positive personal transformation, and consciousness evolution, transpersonal psychology, consciousness research, and the global crisis.

I'm totally a believer in this, and think it's time that we all give our share and do whatever we can to start educating people about what's happening and what needs to be done.

I guess this is becoming my mission and my passion, and I see myself being drawn towards this. I started writing these pieces last night. An unfilled person, one who has many cracks, punctures, and voids, is the one who is constantly struggling to take from his surroundings to feel fulfilled.

Conversely, a person who feels full and content, and does not have the need to take from his surroundings, gives rather than takes, all the time. The first one says, looking within myself, I saw all the answers designed within me, I saw a treasure, an invaluable treasure that I had ignored for so long. I had focused on the unimportant and ignored this treasure. I felt shame, I felt an overwhelming sadness.

I cried. Then I heard a voice. Stop this regret and move forward, the moment you acknowledge it being there is the moment you are born again, start there, start then, move forward, and leave the extra baggage behind. The extra baggage of regret, shame, guilt, resentment, blame, anger, unreasonable expectations, and all the other waste. You are now walking with your treasure. There is no place for garbage. Go for the discovery of your life. Empty your baggage, walk with determination and hope. You will soon feel where it is heading.

And the second one says, like a flower in a vase, like the water in the ocean, like the tree in the jungle, like my soul in this body, like a mother holding her baby, like my tears coming down, like the stars in the sky, I belong with you, I am lost without you. So, come to me, be next to my shoulder, walk with me through this path, the path is long and my legs tired. I need you to walk with me.

Therapist: Well, there is much more than can be seen and has been discovered in this world. When it comes to hateful, harmful, and damaging acts toward others, there are many reasons or combinations of reasons for them. The reasons range from unmet or unattended needs, an unhealthy environment in which one has grown up, and, in some cases, some predisposed biological factors, which all lead a person to not be able to find his or her role and place in life, causing confusion and distress. That sense of distress will be projected onto others, one way or another. This tendency emerges from two systems in the brain. One is the emotional one. The other is the rational one.

Our emotional side usually causes a shortcut response to the problem and encourages immediate action, despite what the long term effects may be. It's impulsive and immature.

The rational side helps us calculate the situation rationally, comes up with a solution that consists of both short- and long-term effects, and has the most productivity. Scientists don't know how these two systems interact or why, sometimes, the two sides take contradictory courses of action. Scientist also don't know how the billions of the neurons in our brains are connected to one another. Until they figure this out, it will be hard for them to understand how perception and behavior are formed. Scientists believe that they will be able to identify a common circuit for everyone, and figure out the functions of specific neuronal pathways, hopefully in the near future. Everyone, however, has different synaptic connections that result from the individual experience.

So, the base is the same, but may produce different reactions. The one thing that we know, working with clients and through our clinical work as psychologists, is that humans have this extraordinary power to be in control of their emotions and thoughts, and even to change a habitual behavior.

That is true even if they were genetically pre-disposed to something. They are still given the power to change it. It may take a lot of effort and determination to go about changing something that has become a part of us for so long, but once we get to a level of self-awareness, and realize the effects in a more multifaceted fashion, we will become more dedicated to initiating the change. I would like, for one thing, to congratulate you for your willingness and your awareness to go through the process. I should say that you have become a transformed person. I have truly enjoyed working with you.

Sara: Thank you doctor. I don't think I would have been able to do it, as productively as I did, without your help.

Being guided by someone who is not just anyone, but whose profession is as a psychologist, and who has worked with many clients similar to me; someone who will look at me without any pre-disposed judgment; someone who will hear me as I am; someone who has unconditional positive regard for me and encourages my honesty rather than looking down on me for sharing my true feelings; just being able to let go of all of my unspoken words; all these have been very helpful.

I feel like a cancerous cell was removed from my body, I don't know, maybe they are those unspoken words, or maybe they are those negative thoughts, emotions, and behaviors that were making the mirror of my being dusty and polluted. I stated the cleaning process, one step at a time, with your help. I'm on my way to purifying. I know that I still have work to do, but I have time, and nothing else to do, and nowhere else to go except to do this. Then come my other passions. I don't know what my true passion is until I have truly been able to purify myself.

Therapist: Remember that I was only able to be of help because you were ready to make the changes.

Now, before the session is over I would like you to take this homework with you for next session. In it you will find a series of questions. You can write them down or just think about them. I want you to think hard about the past few months, and maybe even two years, the changes you have gone through, and how they came about.

Then I would like you to visualize yourself two years from now. What other improvements would you like to have made, and how you are planning to go about accomplishing them? Here is the homework.

Any questions?

Sara: No, not really.

Therapist: Now, let's close your eyes and do a visualization.

The end of the session was focused on Sara visualizing herself attending to all areas of her body and mind, to see whether she could feel anything unusual. This would give Sara a good practice to follow every day during her prayer and meditation time.

Session 13

The next session was the last of this series. It was one of the longest sessions we had. Sara wants to continue therapy for what we call "maintenance." She thinks that she can still benefit from therapy, and I agree with her. We will be meeting twice a month for the next six months and, upon an evaluation, will decrease it to once per month until she feels ready to terminate.

Therapist: So, how was the homework? Did you feel comfortable doing it?

Sara: The questions were very useful. They made me think really deeply. I thought through how fast I've made these changes, how they affected me, my children, and my whole state of being; how the process started, how far it took me, and how much farther I can go. When I look back, I'm truly happy for waking up. I would not trade this awareness for anything. I've become a more reasonable, less judgmental, more responsible, less an idealist and more a realist, less anxious, more peaceful, more confident, and a more complete person.

These characteristics are what I still need to work on. I still feel a mild form of anxiety. Some of it, I know, is normal, but other parts are out of proportion. I don't deny my feelings. I make sure I'm continuously working on it. I have clearer goals, I'm more organized, I've truly come to realize how one mistake can affect me so much, and do the best I can not to make an intentional mistake. I read a lot, and apply the readings to myself. I'm very careful how and with whom I spend my time, and I encourage the same in my children.

I've come out of my deep denial phase, where I thought I was so perfect and my childhood life was flawless, and I was all about pretending and looking like "I have it all." I've learned about my childhood, its shortcomings, and its effects on me. This has helped me tremendously in learning about myself. It's as if, if I have a reason for it, then I can find a solution for it in a smoother fashion. I brought all my denied parts, like my culture, my religion, my parents, and my environment, and started to learn about them, take in what I like, and filter out what was not productive for me and what was nonsense.

I investigated a lot before making decisions. It's like getting the best of everything, not in a selfish sense, but in a truly productive sense. I've become a better mother because I'm able to give more quality than quantity. The one hour of time I spend with my children is better and more beneficial than the ten hours I spent with them before.

Why?

Because I'm more at peace with myself.

I don't pressure myself to do things I don't want to

do, unless there's a good reason for it. I went through the grieving process of what I thought I had, to what reality showed me I had. What I mean is moving from thinking that I had an "ideal childhood life," to having "a childhood life with shortcomings and some abuse." I went from denial to anger to sadness, and now I'm slowly moving to the stage of acceptance. I'm not ready, yet, to have a routine relationship with my dad. I may never be able to do that, but I'm more forgiving than ever. A night does not go by where I don't pray for my dad and my mom, wishing them the best, but I have very clear boundaries about what my expectations are and how much I can give.

I want to make sure I won't get hurt anymore. Deep down inside, if they don't hurt me anymore, I've come to forgive them. I'm in the process of forgiving my ex-husband, even though that's kind of hard, because he still tries to find ways to hurt me, but, it's gotten easier.

I had to go completely out of my own character, who is a peace seeker, to fight back and get what I thought I deserved. That was a truly challenging year of my life. I'm referring to the divorce year. I did everything I could to make sure my ex-husband can't hurt me or my children anymore. I did it with determination, a clear conscience, and hope. I stood by my beliefs, and fought the best I could. I'm building my life. I'm following my dream, one step at a time. I've become successful at my work, I have a couple of good friends I trust and have fun with, and my life is becoming more balanced, overall.

This process is my main priority, I mean the self-actualization process. It's a never-ending story. I also make sure I meditate, pray, exercise, eat very healthily, and take care of myself. I encourage the same in my children. I'm doing a number of charity works that are going smoothly, and I'm writing a book.

For next year, hyperactivity and anxiety are my two main focuses. I still have mild symptoms left in me that I have to work on. I also catch myself in the act of judgment of something I don't know enough about. This is one of the most challenging parts of my work. I still find myself doing that every once in a while. I do understand that preferences are truly normal, but I'm trying to have preferences without judging.

Another thing I'm working on is not making impulsive decisions, I've come a long way with this, but some work is left. After that, I think I'll be ready for the possibility of being open to having a new romantic relationship, or perhaps even marriage. I need to give myself more time with this, since I know I won't be able to make a good decision at this point.

I don't want my fear and my vulnerability to be my guide. I want my pure self to guide me through this process. I'm not even sure whether this is a need or just a fear-signal. I have to investigate it more thoroughly, when the right time comes. All I know is that I'm not yet quiet ready with that.

I see other things, too. I have a more balanced form of emotion. I seem to see the cup as *both* half full and half empty, not just the usual half full *or* half empty. I'm able to find something positive out of a negative situation. I go more with my reason and my heart rather than what others think. I still feel all the feelings, but they're based on more meaningful and simple things, rather than superficial and temporary ones. I can manage my feelings much more easily than before, with the exception of when I see something as unfair to me, to others, or to the world. The sense of anxiety and inner anger comes to me when I sense that unfairness, but the rest of the feelings are just normal human ones. I feel much less sad than before. I have more ways to deal with uncomfortable feelings. I respond to them, rather than denying that they exist. I look for where they're coming from, and what they're trying to communicate with me. Oh, I feel tired of talking now, can I relax?

Therapist: Sure, let's listen to the music and relax. You can help yourself to a cup of tea.

I started looking through Sara's diary while she was relaxing. Sara seems to get into a deep state of meditation when relaxing; she seems to be somewhere else. She usually has a peaceful smile on her face. Sometimes, in the midst of the peacefulness comes a sudden movement. I wonder whether one of her distracting and disturbing thoughts has come to her. When we get hurt as children, growing up with anxiety and fear, and continue the same pattern of behavior that hurt us in the first place, we end up damaging ourselves deeply.

The healing process should be done with love, caring, determination, and focus. During the healing process, the wounds sometimes hurt, and remind us of the memories that caused them. This is a good thing, if one is attuned to them and ready to face these suppressed memories and process them in healthy ways. However, it could be a very detrimental experience if one is not ready for them.

When it seemed like she was ready, we started. Learning about the pattern of personality, the pattern of the behaviors, what consequences our behaviors have had on us, and how we dealt with the consequences, are first steps toward change. In order to do that, one has to start from the beginning of the process. Knowing that the root is needed for growing, we don't focus on the root, but we learn and move on.

Sara's healing process has been a speedy one because of her determined personality, her deep understanding toward self-knowledge, and her education. Her life pattern brought her to a point where she was faced with a traumatizing series of events that forced her into a field that she had always escaped. It seemed like she was in a war with a whole group of people; her husband, her family, and her husband's family. She managed to find healthy ways to deal with trauma, but was worn out by the process.

There was a point where Sara, with all the love she had for her children, decided to actually leave them and go. Not in a selfish way, but the opposite. In a very selfless way, she decided that if she left, maybe her children won't have to experience the conflict between her and her ex-husband anymore. She even started to write a letter about how much she loved them, and how she would be waiting for them in a few years.

It was harder than it seemed.

I asked Sara to share whatever parts of her diary she wanted to. The more I could encourage Sara to release her "unspoken words," the lighter she might feel. I knew that by talking about these deep and complex feelings that have been buried inside her, she would be able to let go of the tension they were causing.

Therapist: Sara, are you ready to start?
Sara: Yes, I'm ready.

Therapist: What would you like to do? Do you want to

go through some of your diary, or just talk about whatever comes to your mind?

Sara: I think I'll read through some of my diary. Let me see, I think this one is good. This is one night during my divorce when I felt like I was in a war that I couldn't handle. I was in the midst of giving up. Then I started to do my routine prayer and went for a walk. When I was able to relax a little bit, I started writing. I knew that by writing I could heal myself. Here it is:

It has been a challenge, my life. It seems like I have designed my life to be hard. I give myself pain sometimes. It seems like I function better with pain. When I'm relaxed for too long, I become unaware of my state of being and my surroundings. When I face challenges, all of a sudden I wake up again and see things more clearly and deeply. Why is it? Why do I take the rough road instead of the easy one?

I started to think about my childhood, how I was brought up in this world, which part of the world I was born in, my environment, my parents, my family, and how each element played a part in who I am today. How each memory is part of me, and until I learn to live *with* it I'm living *in* it, and thus suffocating. It's time for me to feel liberated from the inside. I started to dig in. Who am I? What are my weaknesses? What are my strengths? What limitations do I have? What kind of thinking pattern do I have? What habitual behaviors do I have? I saw the path my life has been taking, because of all those different elements. Now I'm taking a new route, but change is hard. With change comes fear. With fear comes anxiety. But, on the other side of the rope is hope. Never take away my hope; not a false hope, a true sense of hope. My conscience is clear, and I am aware.

Therapist: When there is any form of neglect or abuse, from mild to severe, emotional, physical, or even sexual, there are consequences. Abuse or neglect by a family member seems like a betrayal of trust and an intrusion of boundaries, which may damage the child's feelings of having a safe environment. The fact we should consider is that abuse or neglect does not, inescapably, lead to psychological and emotional issues, and there are many cases of people who have experienced these and have been able to find helpful resources and healthy lifestyle patterns to overcome these difficulties.

There are a combination of factors, like predisposed personality traits, other support systems, and skills used by the individual to overcome these issues, which can change the outcome of the abuse or neglect. Many individuals who have experienced neglect or abuse are able to live a healthy and balanced life. But, for some, it may have intense outcomes that can lead to problems for the rest of their lives.

For example, feelings of powerlessness, loss of control, guilt, shame, isolation, loss of trust, which may lead to further problems in interpersonal relationships and social functioning, depression, low self esteem, dissociative symptoms, flashbacks and nightmares, and physical symptoms. In addition, self-destructive behaviors like smoking, drug abuse, unsafe sex, getting involved in abusive and controlling relationships, alcohol abuse, and eating problems can be another consequence. Sometimes individuals with a history of childhood abuse or neglect may be unable to form intimate and trusting relationships with others.

We, as humans, make self-regulating adjustments as a result of the overall situation. At some point, we might realize our personal responsibility, related to the situations surrounding our lives, after becoming more aware. At other times, one may get stuck in the denial phase and not become aware of his or her own responsibilities, therefore blaming everyone except himself or herself.

One factor to acknowledge is that we're all trapped in webs of relationships. Surroundings affect us, and we affect our surroundings, one way or another, directly or indirectly. To become more aware of our state of being and our relationship with our surroundings, we have to learn to experience the present moment. We also experience our surroundings based on our old attitudes. The person should become aware of that. One has to learn to find a balance between what's happening in the context of the process, rather than content. One has to find a middle ground between actions, thoughts, feelings at the present time, and what might be, was, should be, or ought to be. Awareness is, again, the key. It means that what we perceive, feel, and how we behave are separate from how we interpret, explain, and judge the distinction between our direct experience and secondary (indirect) interpretation. By learning to accept, it gets easier to let go of past baggage.

Sara: I'm sitting in my room, crying my heart out. Who am I, what am I doing here, what is the meaning of my life, am I walking through the right channel, am I doing the right thing? How do I know? My mind seems clouded by all the burdens, by all the force, by all the hassle. I find myself crying, non-stop. I tried to pick up the phone and call someone to pour my heart out, but who? Who would really understand? Everyone seems so loaded with their own life.

I go to my room, meditate, pray, talk to my superior

being, whatever it's called. Some call it God, some call it other names. I don't care what you call it, I call it my hope. The only one I can turn to when I'm lost, confused, sad, and anxious about life and those who have hurt me, intentionally or unintentionally. Don't anyone dare tell me that he doesn't exist, or that I'm imagining. Don't anyone dare take my hope away from me. A hopeless life is not worth living. A hopeless life is a machine life.

I find myself talking to my God, adoring him, begging him for help in showing me my path, guiding me. I find myself telling him that I love him and that I would do anything to connect with him at the deepest level. I find myself talking, praying, crying, making love to my super-being; not a sexual love-making but a spiritual one. I can't explain it, it's beyond words. I see my life passing in front of my eyes. All the hardships, all the blessings, all the ignorance, all the knowledge, all the beauty, all the ugliness, all the good times, all the bad times, one by one. I see them. I feel pain. Such a deep pain. Every cell of my body feels it. I respect my feeling and move on with it, looking for answers, reading through chapters and chapters of information. All this time, it was all within me. I just had to pay attention with love and awareness. I can't stop writing; it's flowing like a spring river. As each word comes out, I feel lighter.

Tonight is the night that I'm evaluating to see which path I need to take after my divorce. No one can understand this, unless they were truly in my heart. They may ask, how could a good and loving mother even *ask* herself whether she should leave her children and move out? I say, you weren't in my shoes, so you could never know.

If there's one thing that I've learned throughout my challenging life it's the fact that you can never judge. Things seem so different from what they truly are. As I write, I have to stop because I sob so hard that I can't see what I'm writing. My words are waiting to come out, but my crying blocks them. Maybe that's why my writing seems shattered. But I want to communicate my feelings as they come, without any addition or subtraction. Let my words be themselves, not what you want them to be. Let me be comfortable with myself. Stop correcting me. Just let me be. Stop judging my writing. Just enjoy them, they are coming from my heart and are trying to penetrate your heart. Be open and receive my words and my feelings.

Tonight is a painful night. I truly feel lonely. They're taking my life away from me. I worked so hard, and still don't know where my life is going. I always wanted to be a good girl, look pretty, be successful, and just make everyone proud. I worked so hard, but was missing one thing. I wasn't being myself. I didn't even know what it was. I was getting farther and farther away from it. I look back at my life, being born in a traditional family, with its own weaknesses and strengths, being emotionally pushed into marrying someone I was so repulsed by. Then I took myself through an emotional roller coaster, denying myself and my needs. I thought having a need was wrong. I felt guilty for having a need, not knowing that a need is every human's survival necessity. In order to grow, we have to have our needs met. We have to feel healthy, emotionally and spiritually. A life lived in anxiety and fear, a life lived in loveless and damaging relationships, is a life wasted. All for what, for who?

When I thought about it logically, I had no reason. I was just weak and lost; lost in a fake world, lost in pretending to be happy and perfect. Sometimes my pessimistic side envies the times I lost and ignores anything good that came out of it. Sometimes my optimistic side tries to make it seem like a good lesson and ignore the harm it's done. Then again, my balanced side steps in, sees it as it is, sees the damages to make sure I won't repeat the same thing, sees the good that came out of it to give me hope for moving forward, and to help me learn from it. Then it all seems okay. I accept it as it is.

I move forward with a clearer vision. I'm more determined than ever to get to my true self and accomplish my task. The task I came here to fulfill. But until I learn who I truly am, I can't really do that. So I lay back, take a step backward from my hyperactive self, take a deep breath, and try to learn to be in silence for a while. Most everyone around me seems so stressed out, so overly anxious, so physically and mentally hurt. They're repeating the same things over and over again; they don't take a moment to see their life as it unfolds ahead of them. They seem to be living for others rather than themselves. It seems like they think that as long as others think they have a good life, they must have a good life. I see more and more people defining life's goal as "to be happy." My definition of life is different. I think happiness is truly accomplished if one can find balance and peace. Otherwise, there's a cost for happiness, and it will always be temporary.

To gain short-term happiness, we have to suffer a lot of pain. One cannot gain one without the other. They go hand in hand. A mother can experience the joy of motherhood only when she experiences the pain of childbirth, and raising a child, with all its challenges. An educated person can experience the joy of his diploma only after going through a lot of sleepless and painful nights and missing out on the fun.

A reasonable person will measure one against another to see what he's gaining for the pain he's feeling, and the challenges he should overcome. It's a form of cost-benefit analysis. I did a cost and benefit analysis to determine how well, or how poorly, my actions will turn out. I tried to add all the positive factors and benefits, and then subtract all the negative ones and the emotional costs. I did this, including my children in the formula because they are a part of me, and my first obligation is to myself and to them. I saw that I will have to pay a lot and go through a lot of hardships, but that, at the end, the benefits will outweigh it.

So, I moved forward with the decision. Some decisions are a one-way street. If you go back and forth with them, you will lose a lot. This was one of them. The question, at the end is, is it worth it? If the answer is yes, and if we trust our reasoning and our determination, then we should go for it.

That's exactly what I did with my divorce. I knew there were many challenges to come. I knew I was divorcing an emotionally immature man who was disturbed in some ways, and that divorcing him might bring out the worst in him. I knew my family, especially my dad, would not be supportive of the concept of divorce. I knew I had to learn to be a single mother in an increasingly demanding world, but was I ready? The more I looked into it, the more I knew I should get out.

Once you have the awareness and the knowledge of something, then you can't go back to the old habits. I knew I had a period of hard times ahead of me, but I was willing to go for it. It was what I truly wanted. With determination, reason, and hope I moved forward. There were times that I thought I couldn't take it any more, the whole world seemed dark, and I felt like I was the only person in the middle of this darkness.

After my divorce, there were a number of men who approached me and were very interested to get to know me on deeper levels, for the possibility of future romantic relationships. In the beginning, fear would overcome me. I didn't think I could trust men any more. I wanted to be by myself, and just focus on making a good life for myself and my children.

I look at the deepness of my soul, and see an empty space. In the middle of this empty space is a blocked pool of light. It seems like this pool of light has always been there, since the beginning of time, and before it. I gaze and gaze, I listen, my heart starts to beat faster and faster, I'm short of breath, I feel like I'm nothing one second, and feel like I'm a combination of everything at another. My mind feels quiet. My thoughts seems to have left me and have moved away, I seem to feel the present, no regrets for yesterday and no worries about tomorrow; just an undisturbed feeling. I take a deep breath, I focus on the pool of light, and all of sudden I feel a bliss which I can't explain; a bliss of being cared for, a bliss of belonging.

All my life I wanted to belong, I wanted to be loved, I looked and looked, and did not completely find it until I discovered this pool of light. I find myself adoring this light. I see that this light is connected to an ocean of light. I feel ashamed for ignoring it, but soon this feeling vanishes. I accept it just as it is. I thank it for letting me connect, and I go on to finish my daily chores. Life is beautiful, with all its pains. I want to live my life to its full potential, and pass the earth with no regrets. I want to be who I came here to be. Time is short. I've lost a lot of time, but it's never too late. I can do it. I have all the love I need right here in this pool. I just need to learn to open it. I will open it and move forward.

Sitting on the bench of my favorite spot in the park, I was looking deeply at the trees while repeating the words, "God is truly amazing." It was such a beautiful day in autumn, a nice breeze of wind, mild weather, with ducks flying from one side of the lake to the other. I was looking at all the beauty around me. I saw different colors and shapes, different gestures and shades. One tree was red, one orange, one yellow, and one green. It was as if every one of them had something the other one did not have, but they were each perfect in their own way. Each of them contributed to the park's beautiful scenery. There was no competition, no harm, nothing negative. Every tree was playing the role it was supposed to play, just living there, looking healthy and giving beauty.

I thought that even though we humans are the most advanced creatures intellectually, on some levels we can't even accomplish this simple task that the trees do. We constantly want to be like others, we're constantly unhappy with what we have, and want more, we constantly want what others have, we don't know what our role is, because we don't know who we truly are. Then I silently started to pray. I prayed and prayed for humanity, for all of us. I felt the pain of ignorance around me, an ignorance that is affecting all of us.

Today is the Day of Judgment. Everything is a learning lesson. I'm looking at my life as if I'm watching a movie. Step by step, since the time I can remember. What led me to this day, what led me choose my life in a way that will be judged and controlled by another human being, I have to present seventeen years of my life in a few hours, and then let the judge decide what me and my children do and do not deserve.

Why did it get to this point? After the clouds of blaming, anger, resentfulness, and all those negative feelings and emotions are removed, I came to see the reality. My passiveness when I was only about eighteen years old, my not standing up for myself, my fears, my helplessness, and my imbalanced sense of idealizing the adults in my life, which gave them the power to choose for me, have all contributed to being married to a man I did not felt in harmony with. Then I chose to stay in a loveless marriage that I did not enjoy, and pretended otherwise. That was yet another choice. I was just imitating others around me. I made a lot of sacrifices, but don't know why I did them or where they were getting me to.

With a true sense of sacrifice comes a feeling of pleasure, but my feeling was resentment. The more sacrifices I made, the more resentment I felt. So, what was wrong with me, why was I doing it repeatedly?

Now, looking back, I see that I chose this Day of Judgment. I was a contributing factor to this upcoming day. I stayed for seventeen years with a guy who I see as mentally and emotionally challenged with monstrous behaviors. Now, he sees this divorce as a game, just because of his mental state, I can't expect him to change his identity; this is who he is. All I know is that I have to do everything within my power to get away from him. I just have to try my best to make the best possible choice for me and my children.

Conclusion

Sara's therapy is ongoing, but less often than before. She reported that she needed to get support to make sure she is maintaining the process. She seems more relaxed, more joyful in her life, less anxious about what she cannot control, and more in control of her life. She also feels a sense of freedom, which is every human being's basic right, but unfortunately this basic human right, too many times, is not respected by others. At the end, it seemed like Sara was able to find the Being she was in search of. It seems like this Being we are all in search of is self-reflexive in both its big and small components. What is projected in it is revealed and shown to the person who projected it.

Sara is a person we all can identify with, one way or another. Through determination, motivation, focus, consistency, and persistence; she has been able to practice the process of self-growth. She was able to step into her unknown, out of her comfort zone, and discover her deeper sense of self.

During her course of life, because of environmental pressures, she had learned to escape and run away from her true self. She did not want to feel her suppressed and painful feelings. The self she came into this world with, the self that was supposed to be nurtured and acknowledged, the self that was supposed to be experienced in full, had been neglected, first by her surroundings and then by herself. Instead, she learned to escape from that real self and spent a portion of her life chasing an idealized self which was nothing more than imagination. Sara continuously and compulsively tried to be this imaginary self, while avoiding anything that would give her a glimpse of the disturbing feelings she had hidden inside for so long. Her identity was more a collection of other people's thoughts than her own state of being.

Through therapy, Sara was able to deepen the process she'd started a while ago. She was able to realize her true self; her strengths, weaknesses, limitations, priorities, and needs, and enable herself to move more in the now rather than the past or future. She learned to acknowledge the past, process it, and move forward with it, releasing her suppressed memories and being in control of them. Living in this state of the present would allow her to be more in tune with her authentic being; her inborn nature. She was able to feel more joy and freedom and lessen her inner anxiety by being more real than ideal. She was able to become more aware, going back to the roots of buried emotions. She was also able to access her deeper and higher emotional state. She felt a sense of inner strength to say no to what did not work for her state of emotional and spiritual well-being, pick her own destiny, and design it the way she chose.

Her lower emotional functioning experiences, like fear, anger, anxiety, neediness, etc., lessened and replaced themselves with the higher ones, like joy, peacefulness, and contentedness. She became what she was seeking.

Sara had falsified who she was for a long time. She had done this in an attempt to maintain some form of connections with those around her to meet her needs, or to gain attention, approval, and security. Through self-discovery, she was able to realize that if she truly learned about herself, she could fulfill many of her needs, including a need for security and approval though herself, by becoming more self-sufficient. This way she won't feel hurt or taken advantage of. This way she will walk into a relationship based on love, not neediness, and she can walk out of any damaging relationship without feeling that she has lost something.

She will be connected to the world and her surroundings, but not attached.

Sara learned not to confuse her essence with her feelings and emotions. Our mind can carry us to limitless areas, anything, anywhere, and make us believe we are this or that, rather than aware beings. We may identify ourselves as American, Muslim, Christian, poor, wealthy, etc. We become lost in a fake state of being, which is continuously fed by others encouraging us to stay in our state of ignorance. It is not until we come out of our denial that we're able to see the reality of our state of being, and to make changes. Let us all pray for the time that awareness overcomes ignorance.

(Self Knowledge Base/Foundation Publishing)
www.SKBFPublishing.com

Expanding your mind, widening your world, awakening your consciousness, and enhancing your life; one book at a time.

SKBF Publishing is a publishing company dedicated to providing educational information for enhancing life styles and helping to create a more productive world through more aware individuals. Our task is to help awareness overcome ignorance. Our publishing focus is on research oriented books including subjects related to education, parenting, self improvement, psychology, spirituality, science, culture, finance, mental and physical health, and personal growth. We try to analyze each book carefully and to choose the books we feel have reliable and valid information based on available research or the credential of the author.

Our mission is to publish information that expands understanding and promotes learning, compassion, self growth, and a healthy sense of self which leads to a healthier life style. Our vision is to make a difference in people's lives by providing informative material that is reliable or research oriented. SKBF Publishing is honored to have the helping hand of a number of scientist, educators, researchers, intellectuals, and scholars working together to review the books before approval for publishing with SKBF.

About the Author

Dr. Rohani Rad has a Doctorate in Clinical Psychology and a Masters e in Applied Psychology. She is a member of American Psychological Association (APA), Virginia Psychological Association, and Applied Psychological Association.

In addition, she is the founder of a not-for-profit foundation (www.SelfKnowledgeBase.com) with the sole task of bringing awareness to a wide variety of subjects ranging from root-oriented understanding of global peace to child abuse. This foundation aims to be a bridge of understanding between the East and the West by generating research-oriented material and awareness.

Dr. Rad is also a researcher, and is actively involved with a number of studies related to emotional wellbeing, children's mental health, and relationships, among others. These studies are performed in both the Eastern and the Western sides of the globe for a broader perspective of factual information.

Dr. Rad has written a number of recognized and up-to-the-point books about the subjects of self-discovery, self-growth, and self-awareness from a psychological perspective. You can find more information about the author and her books on her website at www.OnlineHealthClinic.com

Other books by this author

Book 1: Rumi & Self Psychology.
(Psychology of Tranquility)

Two astonishing perspectives for the disciplinen and science of self-transformation: Rumi's Poetic language vs. Carl Jung's psychological Language.

This book describes concepts like self respect, self liberation, self discipline, self assertion etc in a poetic and psychological language.

Book 2: There is one religion: The religion of KNOW THYSELF.

This book attempts to answer those seemingly ordinary questions of life with deep factual/practical answers. How do I get to my core being? Who am I? What do I do with my religion, culture, environment, family, gender, childhood etc., and how should I interact with these aspects of my identity? I feel like I have no use for some of these concepts. Do I need to learn about them, and if so, why? How do I put meaning to my life? What do I do with my emotional baggage? Others say I have it all, so why do I feel empty, sometimes? Why do I have such an emotional pain and can't cure it? I have so many people around me, so why do I feel lonely sometimes?

In this book there is a case example of an individual who learned about her culture, religion, and family background to ease her self-growth process. An individual who moved from East to West in her teen life, and used her immigration experience as a blessing, considering herself privileged to have had experienced living in two seemingly different countries in her lifetime..She came to learn that this experience had expanded her mind and thought in ways that would not have been possible if she had not immigrated. She also learned ways to learn and acknowledge the aspects of her life that she had escaped from, and found the experience fulfilling and uplifting. She felt a sense of having control over her life, picking what works, getting rid of whatever conditioning does not serve her, and choosing her own destiny.

Whatever we hold, we have to learn about and experience. Only after that we can make an informed decision about letting go of what does not work. If we let go of anything before learning and processing, we are getting ourselves into avoidance and repression rather than freedom. We can't ignore the rules and expect good results.

Book 3:
A concise comparison of theorists including Carl Jung and Abraham Maslow's concepts of the psyche and the self.

Finding a common ground between Carl Jung's general concepts of individuation, wholeness, spirituality and religion and those of Maslow's including his self Actualization and homeostasis concepts. (Out in 2010)

Book 4:
Where is my place in this world?

From egotistical to altruistic way of existence.

This book explains how to move above and beyond one's conditioning to get access to an unrepressed and infinite state of being where one can see that everything is inner connected and there is no separation. To get there one must increase her level of understanding and put her life to practice. The more one experiences life with awareness and knowledge, the closer she gets to her wholeness and that unlimited potential she beholds.